Two if by Sea

Anne-E. Wood

Fourteen Hills Press

San Francisco

The San Francisco State University Chapbook Series anually publishes the fiction or poetry of students whose work shows exceptional accomplishment & promise. The 2006 Michael Rubin Fiction Chapbook was selected through an open competition by an independent judge. Funding for the SFSU Chapbook Series is provided by the students of SFSU through the Instructionally Related Activities Fund.

Competition Judge: Mikhail Iossel

ISBN: 1-889292-12-5
Fourteen Hills Press
San Francisco, Calif.
www.14hills.net

Cover Art: Nautilus Diving Centre / www.nautilusdivers.com
Author Photo: Lauren Phillips
Cover Design & Book Layout: Maria Suarez

The Author gratefully acknowledges the editors of the following publications, where some of these stories have previously appeared: *Other Voices* ("Habits"); *Fourteen Hills* ("Red Lighthouse"); *The Cream City Review* ("The Sentimental Thieves").

Two if by Sea

for my parents,
Jean Crafton Wood
and Charles Osgood Wood

contents

Red Lighthouse

Once he brought us to the Little Red Lighthouse. We packed into the Chevette, the four of us: me, my father, my brother, my brother's friend, Arnie. *This lighthouse,* my father said, *this lighthouse,* he said, *this lighthouse shines its light against the fog, so the boat captains can see the bridge, the low hanging, great gray, George Washington Bridge,* he whispered, *disappearing in the foggy nights. The city,* he said, looking at the skyline wet with rain. *I went once or twice. Once for a play, your mother and I, it was about mice and men—the gunshot shook me before I nodded off, the retard died, and later we walked to a warm café and ate a chocolate cake so moist it sent shivers down my spine. My god, I'll never forget it.*

The whole ride he did not stop talking. About things he did when he was our age. About the bridge and the lights and the river and the city he'd been to once. My father smoked. He smelled like wood. He smelled like beer and mint. It was Saturday and fall. I thought I'd die of boredom, except for looking at the tallness of the cliffs and dead red leaves and the rusty barges. My brother and Arnie tossed a baseball gently back and forth in the backseat—I could feel them eyeing the radio, but my father forbade it strictly. We hardly ever took rides together, and he wanted our ears all to himself.

We pulled up at the lighthouse, down a secret road under the Henry Hudson Parkway. It was red with a broken tower window. The light…what light? It had not been lit for years. Old bottles, wrappers, needles at its feet. It stood there like a person, like the abandoned brother of the bridge, red and dirty and forgotten. We got out of the car.

There are things in this life that will drive you mad, my father said, as he brought us over rocks through soaking weeds to the splintered lighthouse door. *The biggest is the failure of things. For instance,* he said, *the day the shipmen drowned. The day the lantern would not light, the day the fog hung so thick before it, a boat hit the bridge and sank. To think,* he said, *of the men who drowned, whose graves are in that river. Isn't it something? Isn't it the greatest thing?*

My father took off his skullcap. He held it to his heart and closed his eyes. For a moment I thought he was going to sing. His chest lifted under his flannel shirt. *Are you okay?* My brother asked him. That's when I realized my father was big. There was no way to not see his bigness.

Arnie laughed. *You must be kidding. This old crusty thing? A family likes yours would come here on a Saturday and think you've found some kind of palace. You think no one else knows it's here? You think you've discovered this stupid shack? Anyone can see it on their way to work in the morning. A thousand times, I've seen it.*

But my father kept his eyes closed. I wanted to take off my hat, and I would have, had I worn one. The lighthouse smelled of fish and rot and fecal matter and chemicals and sailors, and of all the things that lived and died in the quiet of the Hudson.

Two if by Sea

All my friends died in a shipwreck one winter night.

The telephone rang in our dark and quiet house. I was just a kid then, barely thirteen years old. Well, I had just that day become a woman. I'd been asleep, a hot water bottle resting on the cramped knot in my belly. I could tell with my new wisdom the call meant bad news. I heard my mother shuffle across the linoleum to the phone. What was she doing in the kitchen in the middle of the night? Eating Fritos and buttermilk, of course. She was a gray lump of clay. So was my father, who had a habit of dreaming out loud. I had school the next day. An exam on the Romans. I had taken the textbook with me to bed and had fallen asleep with the Barbarians open on my newly sore breasts. I'd tried to study, but now that I'd bled, none of it mattered. Not the rise, not the invasions, not the fires or the fall.

My mother answered the phone, her mouth full of chips. With one eye open, I could tell it was snowing. One flake appeared in the half-light of my window. The sky was purple, not quite dawn. The kitchen was too close to my bed. I had complained my whole life of my room smelling like pork chops in the morning. I could hear every ping of spoon against cup, every sigh at the kitchen table through the wall. My mother's voice fell to a whisper. *Oh dear,* she said to the phone. *Oh dear, dear, dear.*

She hung up and the house was silent again. I could hear snow fall on the roof. They would cancel the Romans. I was bleeding in my pajama pants. Morning came through the window. I closed my eyes.

I heard her crunch more corn chips and turn off the light. My father guffawed in his sleep from the master bedroom. In his dreams, everything was funny.

The source of my loneliness: A tempest in the North Sea.

Why did they go? What pulled them there? What was the purpose of their travels?

I did not imagine it the way you would: the picture of the ship in the storm—the hail and wind and screams and falling masts, the surrendering craft, the kids' chests rising for air, oars battling the roiling waves, bodies crashing in angry water, the panic, the gasps, the blood.

No. I can only say what I saw in my dreams: still black waters, their sneakers floating in the flotsam, torn sails adrift, rucksacks, soaked journals, the stars. In my head, the bodies weren't buoyant, but sunk like sandbags to the bottom of the ocean. My friends' faces were puffy and blue. They lay in a circle on the ocean floor, bellies towards the surface, holding hands. Abalone sucked slowly at their toes and genitals. Salt preserved their skeletons. I had only seen the ocean once. We lived in Minneapolis. There were nothing but lakes, tunnels, highways, and malls.

They'd all run away and who could blame them? I thought. Who would not have escaped? The fathers had sewn my friends' mouths shut with fishing line. The mouths had sores from where the hooks came through, so when they kissed their first kisses, the kids tasted blood, and felt a hot tenderness on the insides of their cheeks. The mothers looked like basset hounds, moping through the aisles of the supermarkets, sitting in their cars in the parking lots at Target, droopy eyed, bored. What idiot would have stayed when a chance to leave arrived? When there was talk of a ship that could sail them away, what freak child would stay?

Of course I was jealous I wasn't in on their plans. My friends had never told me anything about a ship.

On the way to the funeral, I sat in the backseat as my mother navigated and my father drove. Once in a while they would turn around and say some words about the shipwreck. *It is truly a shame,* my father said. *The way some children go.*

They go and go, my mother said. *Without a thought for the living. The poor parents. To outlive your own child.* She pressed her cheek against the window. Some men on the street were waiting for the bus. They gathered under the bus shelter smoking.

We should give them a ride, my mother said. *It's so cold.*

They smoke. Bad habit, my father said. *How about some music?* He turned on the radio, fiddled with the dial. A cello played Bach. *Whatever you do, don't smoke,* he said to me. *It's a surefire way to ruin your life.*

Not just the lungs, my mother said. *It also stunts your growth.*

The cars stood still. We listened as the radio played.

Words fail, my father said and smiled at my mother. *Traffic,* he said. *The traffic. It doesn't move in this godforsaken construction pit of a town.*

It's the weather, my mother said.

It isn't the weather, it's the roads. If they'd stop trying to fix them, everything would be fine.

It's the snow, my mother said.

It always snows here, my father said. *You'd think people would be used to driving in it.*

People are careful.

People are halfwits! A red car cut in front of us. *Jesus Christ!*

Hallowed be thy name! my mother said. This was the only time I'd ever heard her pray. *Oh, that reminds me,* she said. *We need laundry detergent. On the way back, let's stop at the Rainbow.*

We did not move for eleven minutes.

In those eternal minutes some hideous things were happening all around the world, and in my head, looking at the lights in the downtown office buildings as the car sat stalled, as I breathed onto the window and wrote my name three times in script in the fog, I ran off a skeletal list that did not even scratch the surface:

Minute One:

A plant fell from a twelve-story window in Fargo, North Dakota, hitting a woman in the head, causing grey matter to ooze from her bulbous sagging ears. She did not die but lost her memory. This woman's life had been relatively happy. Only happy thoughts inside that gray. She had been blessed for nothing. All the happy thoughts like snot on the pavement. A man would step here later. He'd wipe the woman's life on the doormat in the entrance of his home.

Minute Two:

A dog ate a snake, disemboweling itself with venom.

Minute Three:

A woman fed her husband a bowlful of lotion, in an attempt to kill him with painful gastric dysfunction. Perhaps it wasn't a practical solution, or a kind solution, or a clean one, but it was a solution nonetheless.

Minute Four:

A girl was born who would be mean to other girls. A boy was born who would be mean to girls and other boys. A loser was born in a world of winners. The loser would, her whole life, be surrounded by those who won, by the thrivers inside this construction pit of a godforsaken cube.

Minute Five:

A couple was married in Tenafly, New Jersey. Later that night, the bride would weep deliriously in a hotel bathroom. Then again, seven years later in a Food Court in a mall, her tears wetting a basket of fries.

Minute Six:

I sat in a car in Minneapolis with my parents and bled.

Minute Seven:

A kid beaten up in a schoolyard. He wore glasses. There were cuts around his eyes from the blow. His underwear tugged up the crack of his ass by another kid two years older named Trip. The crack of his ass would inflame later, a minor skin irritation from the chaffing of skin from the bleached cloth, a little fungus would spread there, causing itch, causing discomfort any time he sat.

Minute Eight:

Trip's father fired the maid after fucking her from behind in the pantry, just two days after telling her he loved her, that he would love her forever, that he would go on holding and loving her until he was dead.

Minute Nine:

Dictators. Torture chambers. They turned on the electric chair in Rawling, Texas. That same minute, minute nine, a father had a dream he ate his children in a soup.

Minute Ten:

Cat fights. Chewed up ears. Dumpster Divers. Dark alley murders. A skiing accident in Vermont. A baking accident in Pennsylvania.

Minute Eleven:

A power failure and the rollercoaster stopped midair in a small town in the South of France. People dangled in their seats, the belts barely holding them back, their faces full of blood.

We found parking. My father sighed. My mother reached over and smoothed down his hair.

They held the memorial service in a theater downtown. It was the only place big enough for the mourners. My parents and I arrived too early, before any of the bereaved. It was a cavernous theater, dark and damp. The entrance smelled like an ancient wet couch. There was a table with flowers on it. There were burgundy chairs that squeaked when you sat in them. We stared at the ceiling and at the weeping chandelier. There were gold sconces that held no burning bulbs on the walls. The mothers filed into the orchestra section, heavy in their winter coats, looking more cold and tired than sad. They had not been beautiful since they were young, but now their eyes were black with circles, their skin the color of lead. Photographs of babies were displayed on easels on a poorly lit stage. I did not recognize the faces as my friends. They looked happy and fat. My friends had been miserable waifs, perpetually starving and on the edge of tears. In the photos, the parents held the happy babies in the air. Fed them cake. Pushed them on tricycles. Blew their naked bellies with their mouths. No one asked me to speak. No one spoke to me. I sucked on some candy as a priest came on stage. The man was old and furrowed his brows.

Oh dearly beloved, he said, his throat shaking.

And for a half second, I really did feel beloved.

We gather here...

And I thought of the sinking ship, pummeled by the wind and rain. The captain was blinded by the white of the moon, which steered him towards the storm.

Let us pray, oh faithful departed...

The priest swallowed. The room could hear the spit travel down his throat.

And I thought of my period. What if I bled more than the tampon could hold?

Peace be with you...

Did their lungs fill with water as they flailed in the night?

And also with you...

Were they chowder for sharks, were hammerheads or mermaids nibbling at their heels? Did they cough snot and salt? Were they thrown overboard, were they lovers before this? Why did they go? Did they sweat rocks together at night, did they tear each other apart, did they remove brokenhearted splinters from each other's feet, did they have their periods? Had the boys been hard?

The priest stood on stage and sang his prayer. I had never heard it before. It was my first funeral. I had never known anyone who had died. There was no pulpit. There was no script or bible. He looked embarrassed by his empty hands, which fidgeted now and then with his robe, and made fists. His voice trembled. I felt as I watched him, he sang his song directly to me. His eyes tore through me and he read the words off my guts. I sunk low in my seat, but couldn't escape. Was it my fault they were dead? Would I turn invisible if I closed my eyes?

Lord God whose days are without end, he began, *and whose mercies beyond counting keep us mindful that the hour is unknown... let the water guide our days on earth in the holy just service in union where you live for ever and ever... with sullen heads and sunken eyes and lungs needing nothing...could it be a secret... here cometh night here cometh end... under ocean salt and seaweed poison jellyfish sucking the dead... a fire in the water come save me Mom and Dad love cabin boy, my nose full of vomit again under water under waves this tumble rip flesh catastrophic weight of sweatshirts, bare chests, the junk underwater, jeans coming off, my socks and dreams like a dance this sinking, yes, they must have prayed, do prayers have wings, does the deep save, are we in water, Oh God I am heartily sorry I have offended you my God who are all good and deserving of my love I firmly resolve with the help of your grace to sin no more and to avoid the ocean... ye masters of pretense set sail on this planet of golden-haired pirates, the communion of saints, the forgiveness of sins, hands holding hurt, walk now, little punks, before we beat the life from your bodies, somersaults, holding on to hair, mine and yours, and stings against wounded upside down bare lungs full of brine, beleaguered shoulders, seagulls smashing, a beach of rock and bird bone, I'm sorry, Lord, make us an instrument of your peace, let me sow love for it is in giving ourselves away that we receive, in pardon pardoned and it is in dying we are born, mother the light, father the dark, your kingdom where you live forever and ever, upside down again, sand washed, rope burned, overtaken, cut up on the inside, cut up, overtaken by intestines, turned inside out for ceaseless lapping of waves, heads dunked, ice in the lungs, revise, repeat, I won't let you go, little dreamer, go ahead and squirm, girl, wriggle around on my scabrous hook, so help me Heaven, don't you see the sea, the blood, the sea, Peace be with you…sing this death song my cute little nightmare…we fell hard, fast, deep into you, you slippery nothings.*

And also with you.

And it was over.

In the silence as the audience prayed, one bespectacled mother across the aisle looked hard at me above her glasses like I was to blame, like I was the one who had ordered the storm. I didn't even know about it, I wanted to say. I would have gone with them, but they forgot to ask me. Trust me, I wanted to tell her. But I looked at the priest and then at the floor. It was black except for dust. There was a pencil, an old parking ticket, a chewed piece of gum. I waited for the feeling that should have been there. My parents and I sat in the back row. They didn't want to show off. We were lucky I got to live.

We were in a theater, so the fathers got drunk on whiskey and put on King Lear in honor of their children lost at sea. They did this in the traditional Shakespearian style: three short fat fathers played Lear's daughters. All of them forgot their lines. The lights accidentally went out. They were nothing but outlines, shadows moving and speaking. Someone dozed in the lighting booth. The fathers stumbled around the stage loaded in the dark. There was no nervousness in the audience, though the men could easily fall. Hurt their backs or their necks and complain for the rest of their lives. You were not watching, they would say to their wives. Our children just dead and no attention paid. No one cared enough to stop the play. The theater was pitch black, but if I squinted I could make out their shadows, and I could hear their drunken boasting, cursing, posturing, in the interstices, in the pauses between the pentameters.

When I think about this now, when I sit here thinking about sitting there watching it…all I could do was listen…*whereupon, whereupon, whereupon…a man may see how the world may go with thine eyes…look with thine ears…has thou seen a farmer's dog bark at a beggar?* That's all I remember. Or I could be making up those words right now. Shakespeare never wrote them. The fathers never said them. You don't remember them. You will look them up later and be disappointed. I invented them just now to make you understand what that day was like. The parents sitting in the dark, my friends dead somewhere on the bottom of the ocean, this play. Lear and his daughters. How long had they rehearsed? It must have been for months before their children had gone. The mothers were silent. Maybe even asleep. My parents sitting next to me in the back row whispered into each other's ears. I saw a bit of my father's tongue slip behind her neck. They were not theater going types. They were hungry and discussing what could be for dinner. A ham or a chicken. Ravioli or eggplant. A roast beef or some hot dish. *Hot dish* my father said. *Hot dish,* my mother giggled. He gently pulled the pearl in her ear. In the low light, I saw it. This is how they made love. This is how they lived. My friends were the lucky ones. From somewhere they watched this and laughed too. They were good people. I'd tell you their names.

But I don't remember their names. I remember the names of our bands: Split Honey. Wheat Thins. Pronto Tonto. Fucking Awesomes. Stalemate. Parker Malone. Is Today Tomorrow? Foreplay. Minor Seven. Walker Kong and The Dangermakers. Feed Me. Folder. Foie Gras. Furious Falstaff. Vent. Poland. Pagan Nights.

Those bands had hard times. We just thought of names walking around the streets of St. Paul. That's where we were but we were supposed to be somewhere else. The Mississippi frozen with a few leaves or a lone glove blowing across the ice. I just remember sleds and their boots. Wellingtons. Doc Martens. High tops with basketball socks. Graffiti in a tunnel. A naked lady on cement. I drew her perfectly with spray paint. The cops couldn't arrest us, we were only twelve. They ticketed the older boys and just drove us home. The Lake Street Bridge. Downtown lit up out the cop car window. Skateboards on our little girl laps. Her hand on my thigh. I did not deserve her love. Was her name Edie? That girl. She didn't know who she was or where she was going. I have no idea where she is now. In a cop car? In a parking lot? With her kids? In an airport? At the theater? Where is Edie?

Twilight. Green and pink neon of the Calhoun Theater sign. We are walking around the lake. Sparklers and lights off the docked boats. It is not winter anymore. It's summer and hot and there are bicycles everywhere. We are holding each other, whispering questions. *Can I fall asleep right here? Do you believe in God? Do you believe me? Do you want to go home? Where is your home, anyway?* They would kill us at dinner. Ground us for the rest of our lives. Who cared? There was nowhere to go.

I left the play funeral to get a cup of hot cocoa. Winter in Minnesota and now they were dead. Hard to breathe in ten below. Feet like bricks in my boots. The people in that town were always surprised by the cold. They fumbled on the corners with shopping bags and kids. They slid a little on the ice. I wore a parka with a hood. I'd forgotten my gloves so I put my hands in my pockets. Cars stuck behind banks of snow. I was thirteen. I walked into the coffee shop. So dull, this stern little town. I bought the hot chocolate from a woman named Grace. *Everything okay, Hon? Your hands,* Grace said as I pushed the quarters on the counter. *You need some lotion on those chapped baby hands.* It was a lonely coffee shop. The customers read and ate muffins, played solitaire. Why did snow make everything quiet?

I walked back into the theater at the end of the play. The fathers were bowing. The mothers clapped softly.

The tearless ride back home. This time, no traffic.

Well, that was interesting, my father said. *You missed the best part.*

I'm tired, said my mother.

I'm hungry. I could eat a horse.

I could eat two horses.

I could eat a barnyard.

You are so funny, my mother said without laughing. She pressed her cheek against the window as she often did in the car. This made her look young.

It's cold, she said.

It's always cold in this town, love. In the winter at least.

At a stoplight, my father reached over and ran his fingers through her hair. I sat quiet in the back seat. I watched his hand caress her scalp. She brought his fingers to her lips and kissed them. I would have sat there and watched it. But my stomach hurt and I closed my eyes.

There were reasons I was jealous of the dead and in the car ride home, I privately listed them. The dead aren't afraid of being caught. They can haunt their enemies, enter the bedrooms at night of the people they hate. Enter the bedrooms of people they love and observe the tenderness of the living's sleep. They sit in reading chairs and watch them breathe. How funny to have to fill the lungs with air. How funny to have to give the eyes a rest from the world. How strange to need sleep when land time is so short. They listen to bands play in grimy basements. They drink beer. They have coffee and scones at the Day-By-Day Café. The dead jack off profusely, what do they care, they have all of eternity, and they know there is no better way to spend time. The dead skateboard down vertical hills, jump from planes, eat wild fruit, walk barefoot in the winter. The dead invade the Minneapolis skyways. They are immune to the cold, but they like the view of downtown. They perch on the cherry in the spoon, slide down the shaft, laugh at the artists filing from the Walker Museum. The dead are like kids. They go to the Rainbow and push each other down the aisles. They don't have to stop. The dead fly. They could dangle from bridges by their dead little feet. Watch the water below and fearlessly dive.

The dead also get bored. All that infinity stretched out ahead of them.

I wrapped myself up in my blankets that night. Because they

kept me warm. Because I still bled underneath them. Because my friends were dead and I was alone but alive and I did feel sort of lucky. I couldn't hear anything except my own breath. I switched off the light. There was nothing to see. The night had just started but soon it would end. So I turned myself over and slept.

The Drinking and the Dead

My grandfather and I were having beers at the breakfast table early one Saturday morning. We had been up all night. He had been talking to me for most of it about the battles he'd fought in the Civil War, though he was born fifty-two years after Robert E. Lee surrendered, fifty-two years after the Battle of Bentonville, where he claimed to have killed two Yankees and a slave using his fingernails, a wine bottle, and one stick. I didn't bother to argue with him. I didn't have the heart to hint that at fifteen, in order to see through his stories, you didn't have to be a historian or even all that good at simple math. As the night wore on, as the pale light came into the kitchen, it became clear he really did believe the South had won.

I sat there mostly quiet, nodding, slowly getting drunk for the first time in my life, watching the old man in his pajamas, smoking like it hurt his face, his fat neck wobbling as he inhaled. I imagined as he spoke, him at eighteen, his head swathed in bandages, crawling through the ditches full of the uniformed dead, and his morphine highs as his limbs bled into the hands of beautiful nurses. On the day the North surrendered, and finally let his people free, he said he had wept.

"I reckon it was the only time during the whole goddamn debacle," he said, "that I let my eyes get a little wet."

They were twinkling a little now, probably from the beer or old age or just from talking.

Above the fireplace, beneath the Stars and Bars, in the room where my brother and I slept all summer, hung hundreds of dollars of framed Confederate bills that my grandfather claimed he would one day get around to redeeming. Then he would sell the house and most likely move North, maybe even all the way up to Roanoke, to escape the torrid summers, which aggravated his diabetes and caused him to have lucid dreams, which led him to wake up and drink.

"I don't like to know I'm dreaming," he said. "I like the dream to cover me, it's the only way I wake up refreshed. Well if it isn't Sampson," he said about my brother who walked into the kitchen. At sixteen, he had long black hair, and the shoulders of a man.

"Uhm. We have work," my brother said to me. Which was true. I tried to hide I was drunk, but almost fell as I stumbled to the stove to make some eggs.

"Jesus Christ," my brother said. "It's going to be a long day."

"Do not take the name of the lord in vain in *my* goddamn house," my grandfather said. "Or next summer you can stay in Brooklyn with your little Eye-talian friends."

My brother rolled his eyes. He'd been wishing he were back

in Brooklyn all summer long. All he did was talk about Brooklyn and write letters to his girlfriend, the Polish Greenpoint Cocktail Waitress.

"If your father had any pride," my grandfather said. "He would have civilized you before he went crawling like a pussycat into his grave. May he rest unquiet."

That was the first and last time he said anything about it. He winked at me and toasted the air with a new bottle. All our empty bottles covered the breakfast table.

"Make me some eggs, I'm starving," my brother said.

"What the hell do you know about hunger?" my grandfather asked him. "You never had to eat rats."

"Here we go," my brother said.

"You never had to taste the guts of a rat. To have its intestines up in your teeth, in the pockets of your gums."

He grinned showing my brother his gums. The color of dust.

"And to love it. To love the taste, not for the taste, but because you know it is keeping you alive. The taste of wanting to live. Pure and sweet. You young kids will never understand the weight of our history, of the crosses we had to bear…"

"You're a drunk. You'll die a drunk. Then the rats will eat YOU. No one will bury your old drunk ass," my brother said.

"Our weight as we strive…to…to…struggle…to be the last ones left."

My brother laughed. My grandfather, teetering, stood up. From where I sat, also drunk, he was enormous. My brother was small next to him. I thought, what if the old man fell forward? I would surely die, crushed under his chest. Slowly, he lifted his foot and slammed it on the table. Two beer bottles rolled onto the floor.

It was a knobby foot. Varicose and blue. He looked at his own foot, trying to find his center. He licked his lips. He pulled up his pajama pant and showed us the scar on his gigantic calf, the interruption of saggy flesh instead of white hair, the way the skin bunched there into tight crusted pink lines. From the back of his ankle to the back of his knee. The fire had happened when he was a boy, just an accident with his robe and the fireplace, just a household accident, we all knew, but it looked like it still burned. Like you'd still feel the heat coming off the leg eighty years from now.

"Laugh, son," he said.

My brother looked at the scar and smiled slowly. We'd seen it a hundred times before.

"Get sober before you come to work," he said to me, putting his hair into his red bandana. "Make yourself puke if you have to. You can't paint houses like this."

He went ahead of me, letting the screen door slam shut.

My grandfather sat back down. It was hot. There were flies. The room was spinning. But I made myself eat eggs. Over-hard. They were okay. My grandfather sat there too and arranged the empty bottles on the table. He didn't talk about the war anymore, or say anything really. It felt weird to be drunk. Not how I expected. I kind of expected a point where you just start crying and telling all your true secrets, all the people you wanted to kill, all the people you secretly loved, like I'd seen all the drunks in my life do. But I didn't cry. I just let it pass through me. Watched the old man eat his eggs.

The Hair of the Dog
that Feeds You

Doctor Willaby stood at my grandfather's bed. I sat in the chair on the other side of the room with a beer and watched the diagnosis. It was summer and quiet except for the fan and the breathing of the two old men.

Evidently Gramps was dying of the shits. The doctor couldn't find anything else wrong with him, not that anyone could trust Morton Willaby. I stayed quiet, but I thought it was strange anyone would take health advice from a morbidly obese chain smoker with a skin disease that caused nasty purple welts on his forehead. He was famous in the county and a few surrounding ones for having sheared the ears off very young black boys during what he called a spell of melancholy in his thirties. I'd heard from the next door neighbor Willaby'd been keeping the ears filed in shoeboxes in his basement ever since the Drought of the Summer of '59.

I didn't really believe it about the ears. Anyway I imagined by now they had shriveled like dried apples and you could not smell them if you went down to his basement.

I'm sure he was not a real doctor at all. He had no office, he only made house calls and he was happy most of the time to be paid with liquor or opium, which my grandfather only occasionally smoked. Still he was the only medical professional in the world Gramps agreed to see. They were old friends. They had been drinking and hating people together since they were kids.

"Besides the diabetes, I can't find a goddamn thing wrong with you," Doctor Willaby said. "Besides the insulin problem, you are the picture of health, fit as fiddle. Except of course for being fat. And your bowels are obviously irritated by something, so I would suggest cutting down on the alcohol and the coffee."

"I never touch a drop of coffee," my grandfather said. "It is the devil's drink. Pass me the KoolAid, son."

I handed him the glass of KoolAid that was sitting on the bedside table. He sat up and sipped, the cigarette still lit in his mouth, and licked his lips. Red Koolaid was all we drank that summer besides beer and Scotch. The old man swore by its healing properties, although nothing seemed to be working now.

He curled onto his side, his head turned away from us. He wore no shirt and his flabby back was beaded with sweat. He always looked on the verge of tears, but today I thought he'd burst out crying. His skin was pink. We had all the bedroom windows open, which only let more heat into the room. We had the fan on, which only blew the old man's farts into my face. I had been sitting with him smelling his rancid farts for days reading novels and watching baseball on television and bringing him what he needed while my older brother painted houses. I had been fired from that job the first week for accidentally showing up drunk. I was better staying at home and taking care of Gramps anyway. He and Tim could not be in the same room, but I was bad at jobs and I didn't mind just sitting and listening. Gramps let me drink. Besides I knew how to cook and I could practice cooking for him, though with the shits he hardly ate. Cooking was the only skill I had. I thought if the old man ever kicked it and left Tim and me broke, I could move back up to New York and work in a restaurant.

"Well," Doctor Willaby said. "If you notice any changes in your stool, anything strange in there, give me a call and I'll come by when I can. In the meantime, eat some prunes and get some rest."

He took his share of opium from the jar on the mantle, carefully folded it into a leather pouch, put on his hat, and left.

"I always despised him a little," my grandfather said. He sat up in bed. "Bring me a wet cloth, Samuel."

About every twelve minutes he would rise to relieve himself. What I remember most about that summer down South, the summer I turned fifteen, the summer of my first job, the first summer I was fired, the summer after my father hung himself from the fire escape in Brooklyn with his belt, besides getting drunk and sitting on my ass and making dinner, was counting uselessly. Tiles, corners, stairs, cracks, the number of shits my grandfather took, the number of times he farted, the number of beers we drank, the number of times my brother rolled his eyes, the days until school, the hours until dinner, the minutes and the seconds until night.

"Probably my time is coming," my grandfather said. "My body is giving in. I've lived a long and turbulent life. A life of war and poverty, of starvation and struggle. I've sacrificed more than any man should sacrifice in a lifetime. Like Abraham, I was asked to sacrifice a son. Like Noah, I've had to build an ark to stay the flood and storm. It was a hard life, but I lived it with dignity and bravery. Now. Come clip my toenails. I do not want to die with ugly feet."

I sat down on the edge of the bed and took one of the old man's feet. His toenails were yellow and brittle at the edges. Around the old man was a halo of that sick-with- the shits smell. A little sweet if not so bitter. With his foot in my hand, I held my breath and clipped the toenails and they fell onto the floor.

"Save those, son," he said, winking. I picked up the toenail clippings and placed them in a neat pile by the bedside table.

"I like to have something to chew on during the ripples of pain."

On his side, he took one of his toenails from the pile table and put it between his teeth. He bit down on it, closing his eyes to show me his pain. This wave seemed to last for about ten seconds. I counted the seconds. When it passed, he sighed and stretched one fat leg out from underneath the sheet and pointed his toes towards the ceiling fan, a little like a dancer. He stared up at his own ugly foot and frowned.

"I'll tell you a secret," he said, a little sadly. "I've never told this to anyone before. But since I'm dying and you are here, I'm going to tell you." He did not lose eye contact with his own foot.

"My whole life I've had these large ugly feet. Shoes never fit me. No wonder I was a troubled youth. Imagine walking around with shoes that don't fit. As a child, my father had to order custom made shoes from Memphis. But that was only when we could afford them. When I was eight, I tried to bind my feet with my mother's stocking yarn. That did nothing but cut off the circulation and made me dream a little harder and brighter than everyone else. It also made me a little smarter because it allowed more oxygen to linger in my brain and not be wasted on the lower extremities. Still I prayed some nights for dainty feet instead of these elephantine bricks. But my prayers were never answered. Sometimes the Lord is mysterious in His cruelty. Do you want to know why I have feet like this, son?"

I shrugged.

"My Daddy was part giant. Do not look at me in disbelief," he said, although I was not looking at him at all, but at the eyelets of my sneakers. "He was a direct descendant of the giants that roamed the earth before the humans. My Granddaddy was full-blooded giant. A man so large he could not fit in a house. He had to sleep outside in the mud with the pigs. Everyone feared his hands, even the preacher. He died before I was born so I never had the opportunity to meet him. But I did not have to meet him to believe the stories of the people he killed with his bare gargantuan hands. Let me see your hands, son."

He held my hand up to the light on the ceiling, a solitary naked bulb.

"Small like a woman's" he said. "Small like your father's." He clutched my hand with his and then was quiet. "Tell me something, Samuel. How did your father play his instrument with such small delicate hands?"

My father wore a suit when he hung himself. I remember looking up to see his feet as his body swung. It was the alley next to Smyth Street. It was winter and the bottoms of his bare feet were blue. My father didn't have large feet. They were small dangling. They were strange, naked under a full dressed suit. His stiff body back and forth like a metronome. I had looked up at the buildings in the city and within seconds it turned night. One two three, two two three, three two three. My father was a bassoonist. When I was a little boy I thought he was a bassoon. Ornery but mellow like a bassoon. He gave lessons in the evenings behind the door. My father's students were the hardest working musicians in the city. They arrived early to each lesson and warmed up in the kitchen where I offered them concoctions I'd invented for their snacks. But they always declined, because they couldn't eat before blowing into their reeds. My brother Tim and I listened to those sad bassoons, our feet up on the radiator, not doing homework. My father hated this country. He often said so. He spat on it from the fire escape with my brother. Spitting contests into the street and into the snow. He hated presidents. He loved maps. He loved my mother even as she walked out the door. He played his bassoon in Central Park on the weekends. He was alone a lot. He was quiet like me except when he was angry. He never got angry with us. He only got angry with his father. One night he drank too much and tried to tell us a story about him. But he couldn't remember the story. Or else it got stuck on the other side of his lips. He took out his bassoon and played. Tim went to bed, but I listened.

When the song was done my father said this to me, "Isn't it dumb trying to be a man in this world?'

I was barely eleven then, so I wouldn't have known, though right then I nodded and pretended I did.

He told me to forget about the story, that the story didn't matter. That all stories end up forgotten. He said listen to the music and he played another piece.

Now Gramps held on to my wrist with the same hand that had just ten minutes ago wiped loose shit from his mammoth hairy ass.

"You know what this means, Sammy? It means there's a little bit of giant inside of you."

I took my arm away and he farted again. This time it smelled a little of smoke. I went into the kitchen to have another beer. The kitchen that summer was full of flies. They hovered over the fruit bowl in the heat. I thought about cooking, but it was too hot. I decided to wait until the sun went down and my brother came home. I drank a skunked beer from the fridge. It tasted good. I liked them skunked in the afternoon. I liked them in the morning too. I'd just learned about the hair of the dog.

Gramps rose to use the bathroom again. He couldn't stand silence. He made speeches from the toilet even when he wasn't sick, but now he almost shouted with the pained gravity of someone who really was about to die.

"Unlike your father, I did not once kowtow to the urge to end my own life. Despite all my physical deformities and the challenges and obstacles that were placed before me."

He groaned a little as he spoke. A gallon of shit hit the water, but all he did was sigh a little and go on. He kicked the bathroom door open wider so I was sure to hear him from the kitchen.

"Do not for a second think that God is not watching you, Samuel. God sees you thinking, Sammy. He sees the spinning of your inner wheels. He sees your contemplative nature, and he knows you are good. You are good to ease me into my death. You are better than your communist brother. But it is only good to waste so much energy on the intricate cogs of the brain. Save the workings of those cogs for when you need them, for when real problems arise. Do not mistake the world's problems for your own and vice versa. Your father was born scared. A pussy from the day he came out of one. Still, I forgive him for his shamelessness. Bring me a cold beer, Samuel."

Why did I take orders from him? There were moments when I did think of killing him and I could have. Without me, he could easily starve. I could easily place a pillow on his face and push a little in his sleep. I could easily drink with him one night and switch to water as he drank himself to death with Scotch. One, two, three, bottles of Scotch and he'd hit his head on the floor. We could take the train back to New York one morning and leave him to rot down here. Still, I brought him the cold, skunked beer and handed it to him as he sat on the toilet. My grandfather, grim and naked on the toilet with the shits. His face red with dehydration. His boxers at his heels. The smell of ass and bad beer on top of all the heat. Thank God his great belly hid his old man's withered cock. I would have rather died than see it.

"You are the salt of the earth," he said, winking, as I gave him the beer. It was time to make dinner. I went into the kitchen and got some onions out of the fridge. I started cutting up the onions on a cutting board. My eyes filled up. The onions always did it. I got this raw chicken I'd bought that morning and slathered it with butter and garlic. I started making a sauce with pepper and lemon. I got out all the bowls I needed. I drank another beer, to get the edge off. I made the sauce noisily and banged some pots and pans. I was beginning to feel drunk again. That was what that summer was like. It was just getting drunk and listening to my grandfather. He was shouting now.

"You'll grow up to be a man I'd have been proud to raise for a summer. I know it's only been one summer, but since I raised my son...for better or for worse...for cowardly or for bravely...for...meekerly or for strongly...for holy or for unholy...I have raised the two of you vicariously...From me to my son, to his sons...from my son to his sons to your sons...we are a world of sons, a history of sons, connected forever, what a long life in this world. Oh God, will it ever end?"

He let loose his stool again.

"Connected forever," he continued, "through illness and through death. We all die," he said softly. "In our lifetime, rich or poor, male or female, African, Chinaman or White, we all have the painful watery shits at some points and we all end up in the earth. That is the way of the Lord Almighty Halleluhjiah Amen Praise Be."

I thought about leaving. Just walking out the door and going for a walk. He was drunk enough not to know. He was mostly interested in hearing his own voice and he didn't need me there for that. But I didn't leave. I thought I'd help him to the bed again.

His body swayed on the toilet. One and two and three. In a few minutes, he would pass out. I thought of just letting him do that right there. But then I thought he could hit his head on the tile and there might be blood. I couldn't handle blood. So I grabbed the old man by his chest and helped him up from the toilet. Something happened to me right then. My body did this thing called holding Gramps, but my heart was somewhere else. I didn't see the stream of toilet paper clinging to his ass. I couldn't smell the eggy shit stench of the toilet. And I didn't look to see the amber clotted mess smeared on the seat. I just held my breath and held his chest. I felt my stomach slosh up to my throat. I was drunk and going to lose all the beer I'd had. I helped him walk, his pants at his ankles, from the bathroom to the bedroom. One step every thirty seconds. We were teetering. One wrong move and we would fall all over each other. That short little walk, my sneakers stepping on his feet, the both of us kind of drunk and him leaning on me. Well it just felt like a pilgrimage. I thought we'd never reach the bed.

"If I could just take you with me," he said, clutching onto me.

He held on tighter to my shoulders. Now his breath was on my face. Halitosis from the bacteria in his gut rising to his throat. There was a little death inside that hot old mouth. His chapped white lips almost touched mine. His wet whiskers touched my cheek. There was a little spit on his chin. I imagined going with him, the way he wanted, wherever it was. Into the sky or into the mud. His body would get blue with rot and he didn't care if mine did too. A rotten man and a rotten boy. As long as I was lying with him, he was fine. I held his shoulders and pushed him away. Finally, we reached the bed. He collapsed onto it, diagonal, facing the ceiling. He let out a long sigh.

"How do you feel?" I asked him, after a pause. It was the first time I'd ever asked him that. He looked at me sternly.

"The pain comes in waves," he said. "In sporadic waves of intense size and force. Then comes the movement of liquid waste through the large intestine, the blind gut, the rectum, and out the anus, which burns when the episode is over. Then there is a rather pleasant pause. A flash of reprieve orgasmic in sensation. For what is an orgasm if not the cessation of pain? What is death if not the cessation of dying? To come is to die a little. To shit is to die a little. Therefore to shit is to come. I should be happy. I should be thankful for these last hours on the can. And yet, yet, and yet...I see doves," he said, out of nowhere. "I see doves and stars, and I know the end is near."

The old man shut his eyes and evidently fell asleep. I pulled the sheet over him, though it was still hot. We sleep better under covers. I don't know why. I think we're better hidden. Before I shut the door, I took one last look at him. Well, it wasn't the last. I'd see him again, but I wouldn't look. I wondered what my grandfather dreamt of sometimes. What dreams bothered him the most. And if he really was scared to die. If he believed what he believed, that there was a Doomsday. Was he afraid to meet the day of reckoning with his trousers at his ankles? If there was a God, He'd take one look at my grandfather and do one of two things: either He'd send him straight to hell, or He'd start laughing His ass off. Or maybe both. The room was yellow. The light came in through the window and made it even yellower. The fan was still on. It was okay. It was an okay room for dying.

I took his cigarettes from the bedside table and went outside to smoke. There was Timmy, coming home from work. He looked like he'd been through hell. His red bandana was wet. Painting houses in Tennessee for a summer was a like a little special slice of hell. He looked bedraggled and spent. For a second, coming up the road, he looked like my father.

"Dinner ready? I'm hungry as fuck."

"Not yet," I said.

"I think you are the laziest son of a bitch this side of the Mason Dixon. Here's me working my ass off all day, and I come home to you smoking on the porch."

"It'll be ready. I was nursing Gramps. He's still got the trots."

"For fuck's sake, man. The whole house will stink."

"Yup."

"There go my chances of getting laid tonight. I'm not going to have my girl come over here now."

Tim never had any chances of getting laid. He had muscles, but he was ugly. But I would never let him know that because I loved him so much. You've got to love the ugly. Evidently, you've got to make them dinner too.

Dr. Willaby came by again at eight. He had the ghost high look in his eyes from the opium. He opened the fridge, but didn't find anything in there to his liking. He helped himself to some KoolAid. I could have invited him for dinner, but I was with Gramps on this one: I couldn't stand the guy. I told him about the stars and the doves.

"Delirium tremens," Dr. Willaby said. "That kind of drunk will live forever. There is nothing to be worried about."

I burned dinner. I think because I was drunk. Timmy didn't help. He just sat outside on the porch smoking cigarettes. It was okay because he'd worked all day.

Besides being burnt, there was too much garlic in the chicken sauce. That's what Tim said, though I thought it was pretty good. And to tell you the truth, he looked like he was enjoying it. We ripped the flesh off the chicken with our teeth, and played a game Timmy invented where you had to spell your name by throwing bones on the grass. If the bones landed and didn't spell your name, you had to drink. It was an exceedingly retarded game, but we didn't care. We were fucked up on that bad beer. What was great about having a lunatic watch over us was the mess we could make. There were dishes and bottles and bones all over the kitchen floor and the porch and the lawn. We took out the radio and listened to this one stupid song that played over and over again that summer, it was by some husband and wife country singing team and the refrain went like this:

Ain't got chicks, ain't got lips, ain't got money, it ain't funny, is this the land of milk and honey?

And when it played we did imitations of our grandfather. Tim did it best. Now do Gramps at a ballgame. He'd totter around the porch like a hippo catching a ball with its teeth. Now do Gramps dancing the Macarena. And Tim as Gramps the hippo would do that twirly thing with his arms and he would raspberry out the loudest earth shaking fart you ever heard, in the whole history of faked farts, before jumping off the railing of the porch and landing on a pile of chicken bones and beer bottles and looking up at the stars in the Tennessee sky.

"What if the old man wakes up?" I asked Tim.

"Let him."

We turned it upside down that night, man. And we ate like orphaned princes, like kings. We were the descendants of giants, and we were starving.

Accidental Encounters

He belonged to the sad men. When the ambulance brought him there, he wanted only to sit in the dark. The night light of the boy dying next to him hurt his eyes. He didn't notice the kid right away. Only the sound of him still breathing there. His slow sound, the whining for his mother, the quiet blood boiling sleep. The wheels on cold tile, the rush of panicked time, beat. Suitemates for the week in the stiff hospital. On the turnpike he'd swayed towards the end of the world, meaning towards the sea and cliffs, hurling backwards on the highway. It was a dream but no dream. He did not remember but lay there how many hours in the dew. Nothing came to his rescue. Not a sound. Three mean spirits came to spit. One in the shape of the moon. One an eagle licking its own wings. One a paramedic named Appleton, too fresh for this job. His head like a water balloon and the teenager's wide dumb eyes. Not quick enough, his fingers slipping. This is the work of the fast and fierce. Do not come around if you have large hands or if your eyes wander. Morning double sirens sped, he was part of the sad landscape, the embarrassed cars ignored him. Then he woke to see little fingers dangling off the side of that bed. Where's your cut gut? Where's your mother? How old are you today? How many fingers? You have a beautiful brain. What do you see in this picture? A bicycle? A pair of antlers? Rabbit ears? Was it a mountain? Who is looking after you? Do you remember your name? Do you know how old you are? Say your name. Under the silence: falling paper. He will be swathed. His feet will be washed. Tomorrow night he will find a quiet place to read, when his head is sorted. In between the tawny days, go swimming like they used to. In the black lake with the mossy dock. Washed pieces of fruit in our pockets. I'll fix it for you. The other he tried to pluck his nose hairs in his dream. They glistened from the tears. On his hot little cheeks. They brought him yogurt for his burns. Extracted concrete from his back. He was himself and the boy. He looked at himself, the solemn boy. The almost dead. Took out the glass with tweezers. The boy screamed from not knowing, not from pain. It's okay, little man. We're all warriors here. Everybody in here, we're all on the same boat. Sailors, you know. Pirates. You are not alone or lost. After this we'll go back to the water, dive to the bottom of shipwrecks, eat the treasures. Blankets around me please. Around and in between and beneath and straight through my quiet gentle head.

The Flood

"And then, during the fire, do you want to know what happened during the fire? During the fire…during the fire as I stood on the ledge, I shook out my dress, the one my uncle had sewn for me, and looked at the pit below, and had to decide, should I jump or burn in the flames, should I find the boy I was looking for, or should I think only of myself…Never mind. You're not even listening."

It was four in the morning and I was trying to fight sleep. My head hurt. I had been lost in dreams of my own. Sweet, restful dreams, the kind that take you away from your life, the kind too beautiful and pointless to try to describe.

"You never listen to my dreams," she said. "You never, ever listen. You think I don't know, but I do." She leaned over and turned on the bedside lamp. She shared my pillow and looked right at me. Her eyes were the pink eyes of pigeons.

"I can tell that you're not even looking at me," she said. "I can tell by the way you're looking at me, you're not even looking at me."

"I'm listening," I said. "I'm listening now." I turned my head away from her and towards the window. The night bus went by on the street below. It was raining hard now. She started again.

"And the eagle had such awful claws. I could feel them digging into my shoulders. But it wasn't an eagle entirely. It was an eagle, but also an attic. But not quite an attic, an attic in the shape of a wilted penis, but not even so much as a penis as a grey, low-hanging cloud..."

I listened to the episodic plots of her dreams. To the transformations and amalgams and symbols and boundless geographies, to the strange cities and impossible architectures she created in the recesses of her head, in her memory's intricate folds. I listened to her father become her brother become her ex-lover, to the store keeper who was a wolf who was her old gym teacher she had kissed, to the abandoned babies at her doorstep, to the earthquakes and pregnancies, lost teeth, blindness, diseases, found money, the dogs of the ballerina next door, how they gnawed on her prom dress on her way to the gym, fatal car races, stinking elephants rolling on the living room floor, screaming rats in her bathtub, quietly I listened to the planes crashing over Egypt, to the long lost grandmothers, to the story of her flight over San Francisco with a new sprout of maggot-munched wings, to the strangely hot sex with unlikely partners, once with one of her eighth graders, for instance, the smart one she'd always despised, how his braces cut her lips and made her come as she bled, another tryst with the barista at her favorite café, she was thick but firm, she'd described, and I listened, so quietly, I listened to her dreams.

Shut up and let me kiss you, I wanted to say. I have a painful erection despite the dullness of this conversation. But instead, I said how interesting, how traumatic, how bizarre. How immense the life is inside your tiny head. Sometimes I asked her to repeat herself, did you say the man's face was blue? Blue, did you say, and was he playing the cello or the violin, I asked. I smiled at the funny moments, scrunched my forehead in the difficult sections. Once I'd squeezed a solitary tear from my eye and let it fall.

"And then I woke up," she said now. "What do you think about that?"

Another bus went by.

"You weren't listening," she sighed.

"I was listening."

"It's over. Completo. The End. You don't care about my dreams. You were looking out the window. Probably wishing you were on that bus. I wish you were on it too. I wish you'd jump out the window in front of that bus. I wish its wheels would crush your bones."

I found a cigarette on the nightstand.

"I hate when you smoke in bed," she said. "Forget how disgusting it is. It's also dangerous. You wouldn't care if this mattress, this room, this whole house burned to the ground. You wouldn't care if my face burned. If all the skin of my entire body were crisped. That is how self-centered a man you are. It's really quite horrible to be with someone who only thinks of himself."

How it rained that night. I thought the city would flood. And then we'd have to make rafts. But how would we make rafts?

We'd use the furniture of this house. She'd take the bed, I'd take the couch, or the dining room table, and we'd go rafting down the streets of this town, I thought. We'd use our coats as sails. Everyone else would drown, but we'd go rafting through the city under the sky...

"You know what the worst part was? The worst part about the volcano," she said, "was that it wasn't a volcano, but a giant cup of soup, with enormous noodles in the shape of letters bobbing up and down in the lava, and I threw you the letter P so you could use it as a life preserver. I was trying to save you, I swear, in the dream I was trying to save you..."

...just drifting like that under the stars. We'd wave at all the people standing on the roofs of houses, clinging like fools to bridges. Imagine what the city would look like covered in water. It would look like Venice, I thought. It would look like Venice scattered with floating corpses. But we would not be among the corpses. We would be among the sailing. We'd sing songs to each other about life on the water. With the rest of the city dead, we'd sing.

"And then," she said "when the tarantula opened its mouth," she said, "it whistled, Gershwin, or something like Gershwin, and we were back home again, except our house was really the Guggenheim, in the shape of a cone, with those staircases, endless, spiraling, dark, that's when the whole thing really turned into a nightmare, I knew none of it would end, and I knew I was dreaming, but I refused to wake up..."

All night like that, weaving up and down the streets, I thought. She would not sleep and therefore she would not dream. And if she dared to shut her eyes and go to sleep, if she dared for one second to go off into those dreams and felt the need when she awoke to speak about them, if she even opened her mouth to say and then and then, I would push her off into the water. I'd watch her drown. I would not lift a finger to save her. Finally, I'd be alone. All by myself with the city and the water, smoking and sailing in the quiet of the night.

"What are you thinking about, for Christ's sake?" she said.

"Nothing."

"Your lips are moving. It's scary."

"It's just I love you," I said.

Another bus went by. It seemed like the buses were never on time on any street but ours. On any other street in that city, you'd wait an hour at the minimum for a bus to heave its way down the road, and you'd always decide it would have been better to walk. Or crawl. On our street, a bus came every two minutes at all hours of the night. Most of the time empty of passengers. A solitary driver doing his job.

Now the two of us smoked, propped up on pillows.

"I hate the rain," she said. "And I despise this city. It reminds me of a tomb. Everyone thinks it's beautiful, but that's because they're nuts. It's done. It's completely lost its kick. The people here are zombies. All they do is drink coffee and talk about their work. I don't know why they have heads. I'm always cold. See? Feel my hand."

I held her hand in mine. She was right, her hand was cold. I kissed the back of it and placed it under my pajama pants. She pulled it away.

"And how are we supposed to make love with all those loud buses going by? Where's the romance in that? If you loved me, you would take me away. But you're not even listening," she said.

"I'm listening," I said.

She closed her little eyes. I looked out the window again, at the grey, wet street. And what would it be like to drown? To breathe water into the lungs, to feel the chest tighten, the stomach constrict, to gulp into the mouth the flood of the city, to feel the waste of the streets on the inside of the cheeks. Her face would turn blue and the current would spit her out into the ocean.

"You'll be food for sharks," I said. But now she slept. I rested my lips on hers. "Do you hear me?" I whispered.

Nightwatcher

Who belongs to these boats? They do nothing but knock against each other on the docks. They are rusty and no one's. Probably some kids sneak on them at night to drink beer, smoke, and kiss. Two boys who dream of sailing. Or a girl and a poet grinding starboard. Or all four of them, looking for some early trouble. The stinking river, the lit up bridge, the bottles, the curious tongues. The old highway and the open city. I remember what it was like, no one has to remind me. But on school nights, nobody squats on them. Just me sitting here on dry land, filling them up with ghosts. I'm not scared. I'm collected. They're all my own. I'm just facing Jersey. It's heartbreaking in the dark. Kind of like a sullen moon, blue and gleaming, doing its thing, looking back at me, down on me, over me and all.

Habits

I'm watching my mother from my window.

It's late at night and she's outside in the backyard, alone, pacing. She isn't angry or worried. She just walks slowly, back and forth in straight lines. From the flowerbed to the swing. From the swing to the fence. She talks to herself as she walks, whispering words I can barely make out. From the window where I watch and listen, I catch these words: *My sons. Spoon. Lightning. Coats.*

I write down the words I hear in my black book so I'll remember them later. I watch her. I go downstairs in my pajamas, very quiet because my brother and my dad are asleep. I open the sliding glass doors. It's summer and the grass is cool and wet. I stand behind her and watch her pace around the flowerbed. For a few minutes, I stand there. Besides the whispering, besides the crickets in the trees, besides my mother's feet crunching leaves, there's a strange kind of quiet. She wears a nightgown with birds on it. Her hair is long and in two braids. If there were a moon, the moon would light up her wide face. But tonight the sky is black.

"What are you doing? Is something wrong?" I ask her. She isn't startled. She doesn't turn her head.

"Go back to sleep, Logan," she says. Not strict, not mean, just above a whisper.

My mother isn't crazy. She has a normal day job as a substitute teacher. Her husband teaches history at the high school. She has three boys, two fifteen, one twenty-two. The oldest one has some problems, but he's had problems forever and doesn't live at home, he shouldn't keep her awake pacing like that. She has a cat she loves. Sometimes she takes painting classes. Watercolors of beaches and buildings fill the rooms of our house.

I watch her. She paces. She stops whispering words, but she keeps pacing. My mother is young, had all her kids early, but in the dark, walking slowly like that, she looks about eighty years old.

"But what are you doing?" I ask. "Are you okay?"

She smiles like it's all right, and I go inside.

I stare through the glass at my mother in the dark. I pour myself a cup of milk, closing the refrigerator lightly so it won't make a sound. I go outside again.

"But what are you doing?" I whisper.

She says nothing. I listen as I hold the milk. Dogs bark from far off and the neighbors' sprinkler turns on.

It's on the tip of my tongue to tell my twin brother. I almost wake him to tell him. I look at him asleep in his bed, snoring. Derrick gets so hot at night in the summer, I can tell. His face gets sticky with the sweat, and I can smell him, I'm starting to notice.

Salt and underarms. And the Old Spice shaving cream since we just starting shaving a few months ago. I can smell him even before I walk in the room. Do I smell like that? I doubt it. We don't wear matching pajamas anymore like we used to. We don't have long talks like we used to in the middle of the night. Derrick under the glow-in-the-dark moon he's had above his head since we were eight. Derrick, a fifteen-year-old who still has Thundercats sheets. I changed mine years ago. He falls asleep before me and sleeps hard like he won't wake up until the alarm goes off.

He's just like me, only not really at all. Now everyone can tell us apart.

On Sunday night, Mom and Dad go to an AA meeting and leave us alone in the house.

There's a closet we're not supposed to go into down the hall. Derrick looks at the closet like there's something inside it he needs. It's like he can't not think about the closet. I borrow the best video game from our neighbor. I buy a pack of Luckies for later. I tell Derrick the videogame rocks, it's the one where you are the skateboarder Tony Hawke and you skate through shopping malls and grind down long banisters and spin off cars in parking lots. Derrick and I play and I almost beat him, but I know it isn't because I got better—it isn't because I've got good moves. I don't, I suck. I know it's because he's thinking about the closet.

"Logan, let's look at it," he finally says.

"What about the game?"

"Forget the game."

We go to my dad's office and find the file where the key is. We go through the hallway to the long peach door. Inside the closet there's a shoebox full of Hustlers, an American flag folded into a triangle, a knife from the Civil War and a long white robe with a hood. That was my grandfather's Klansman robe that he wore when he was alive, when there were many Klansmen. He's dead now. Derrick puts the robe on, and pulls the hood over his head. The hood's too big for him. The robe trails behind him like a bride's dress. His Nikes stick out from under it.

My grandfather shot a man in the head once. That was in Tennessee a long time ago. It's a bad story for my father. He never spoke to my grandfather after that. After he stopped speaking to him, he started drinking. Then he got married and went to AA, became a Christian, and he's been sober for twelve years. A history teacher. Instead of whiskey or gin, he drinks eighty million glasses of water a day, like his life depends on it. Like he'll dry up if he doesn't. There's the water drinking and the praying. I don't know how he keeps a job in between.

"Boo!" Derrick says, his arm around my neck, his two fingers at my head like a gun.

"Fuck off, asshole."

Inside the hood, he sits down in the hallway, reads the pussy magazines, reaches his hand inside the robe and starts to jack off, right in front of me. His adenoids make him breathe heavy. He sounds like Darth Vader under the hood. I don't know if he'll come all over the robe. I don't stick around to find out. I take one of the magazines, which is why I agreed to open the closet in the first place, and go to the bathroom to jack off like a normal person.

Pretend it's a scary movie. It's late at night and we're asleep in bed. My grandfather knows we were in the closet. He saw us from the yellow photo hanging in the hall. The one where he's in his twenties, standing outside a barn with his dog. Why my dad keeps a photo of the father he hates hanging in the hallway, I have no idea. Our grandfather jumps out of the photograph, puts on the hood, takes the ax from the porch, creeps up the stairs, finds us in our beds and starts swinging and chopping. Blood squirts out of our ears and eyes. We die in our beds, our blood drips from the walls and ceiling, our arms and legs broken and scattered all over the room, our heads roll around on the carpet, and we can still hear our mother pacing outside in the yard.

I can hear her right now in real life.

"But what are you doing, Mom?" I whisper to the wall. "What are you doing?"

Like a retard, Derrick forgets to lock the closet and Dad kicks his ass when he gets home. I watch from the stairs. Derrick is quiet against the wall. Doesn't yell back, doesn't even cry. Just stands there taking punches in the gut from my giant father.

Late that night, our dad comes into our bedroom room. He turns the knob quietly because he thinks we're asleep. He breathes hard, the way older guys do. He checks the alarm, makes sure it's set. He turns on the nightlight on the stand between our beds. I stay under the sheets, peeking out just a little. He doesn't say anything. He sits on Derrick's bed. Quietly in the dark like that. He drinks from his water bottle, gulping it down the way he does. He takes the back of his hand, feels Derrick's forehead, and kisses him on the cheek. He puts his arm around Derrick and holds him. I try not to listen to my father holding Derrick. But they're both so close, it's hard to not. He holds Derrick tonight and starts to cry. Jesus, Dad. I don't know how Derrick feels about being held by his dad like that at fifteen years old. Better him than me. I don't know how he feels about his dad crying like that in front of him. I wonder if he's awake. He must be awake. He's a hard sleeper, but my father's big, breathes deep. And how could you not know if a big thing like that is hugging you, crying the way he is? How could you not wake up? But then I think about Derrick awake. Cringing probably. Hoping I'm asleep. Why doesn't he say something? Like, Dad, get off. Get the hell off. What the hell are you doing, Dad? I can just imagine what it feels like. My dad with that cheese breath crouched over you, crowding you. Or maybe Derrick likes it or something. Looks forward to it. Like it's some father-son bond they have that I don't and never will understand.

In the kitchen I write down the words my mother says in the black book. The book is old. My big brother Teddy found it in the attic and gave it to me. It's leather bound and it was blank when he found it and the pages on the inside are crisp and yellowed. I always wonder who bought the black book and what it was for. Who forgot about the black book and how did it end up in the attic? I write down the words my mother says when she paces in the dark backyard. I write down the same words ten or eleven times then think of other words that remind me of the words she says. The words are lists, not sentences. The words are just words. Like watch. Like grass. Like storm. Like water. Sky. Dogs. Birds. Hair. Night. Summer. Bridge window brother dancer timber tin head tall fist fight slow blend kite radio quiet tell mad dinner girl coat hat forget gin tinkle bat. Lists of things, sometimes. Sometimes phrases. Shit, this walking in the dark's been going on so long, I have pages and pages. Just words. The ones she says and the ones that come to me. I don't know why I'm into it, I just am. If you say a word over and over again, you forget what it means. Take the word nose. Say it a hundred times fast. You won't think of a nose. You'll just know this sound. Same with the words on the page. They don't mean anything over and over again. But I like the way they look. The lists of the blue words on the yellow pages.

On Friday night, my big brother Teddy and I walk across the George Washington Bridge. They say muggers stand on the landing sometimes. Wait for bridge walkers to walk at night. They grab you and tell you to give up your money or they'll throw you. A few times a year it happens. As far as I know, no one's been killed. No one's been dumb enough to test them.

Down below, the Hudson stinks. We can smell it from all the way up here. That sloshy, rancid mess.

"A guy at my school jumped in once on a bet, in the middle of winter," I say. "They had to pump black shit out of the insides of his lungs for days later. Oily chunks in his stomach. Eye and ear infections, diseases on his crotch."

"He won the bet, though, huh?" Teddy says.

So few cars cross over since it's the middle of the night, but there are enough so it's not too quiet. The bridge is great big steel gray with crisscrossed patterns all the way up. My favorite bridge in the world. The guy who built it originally planned the steel to be the skeleton, and was going to lay granite over all that steel. But the steel looked so good, all raw and shiny silver, everyone decided it was done.

I feel about this bridge like how I'd feel about God, if I believed in God. To me, it's like this big grandfather lying down asleep between New Jersey and the city. This majestic old man. Sometimes I forget how much I love it, I cross over it so much. I forget to really see it. But tonight's a night when I notice it. The two of us walking, the hot summer night, I see it. Hey, old man, I want to say. Hey.

Teddy's long and doesn't look like the rest of us. He rides a motorcycle and has hair so black it's almost blue. He wears a black leather jacket with an army green tank top underneath. Teddy has tons of enemies and makes new ones everywhere he goes. When he was younger teachers hated him, bosses hated him, girls hated him. They all still hate him. Imagine knowing the world hates you. What's the point in trying? My dad won't even let him in the house except on Christmas and Easter. In between the holidays, he prays for him. God bless Teddy may he find the path of righteousness from which he has strayed. May Jesus come knocking on his door. May the Lord have mercy on his lost and wandering soul. May he learn how to get a real job and pick up after himself. I can't decide if I like Teddy or not. Every time I want to hate him, he does something that shows he cares.

Teddy climbs over the rail and holds on from the other side.

"Shit, Ted." I say. I can feel what's coming.

When he does shit like this, he gets mesmerized, like he's in a trance. He presses his lips together and bears down on his teeth, and the muscles of his jaw tighten and it's like he's pressing from deep inside of him, he's pressing, and he shuts his eyes and it's like he goes away to some other world, and looking at him, you can tell he gets this weird pleasure out of it, and that's when I know it's not about putting on a show for me or anyone else. Like, Teddy does this when he's alone and no one else sees. He doesn't care about anyone else, what they think, or what they want from him. He just loves this thing he does. I don't know what it is, the height, the danger, maybe it's like he thinks he's overcoming something. A guy builds a tall bridge and the whole world knows you're not supposed to dangle over its sides like an asshole, the whole world understands about gravity, and there are these laws you're supposed to obey, like you're supposed to give respect to this bridge, you're not supposed to put yourself in danger like that, the world is dangerous enough with muggers threatening to throw you off, and it's because of guys like Ted that tall rails and fences and locks exist everywhere you go, to protect idiots like him from their idiotic selves.

Just when I think he can't be more of an idiot, he does this even more completely idiotic thing. He lets go of the rail with one of his hands.

"Shhh," he says.

"What the hell are you doing?"

"Try it."

"Come on."

"No, really."

"I don't want to try it."

"It feels good, Logan."

He lets go of his other arm, and he's just holding himself up on the George Washington Bridge *with his feet* between the bars, the toe part of his boots wedged and holding him, his knees resting on the steel, but the rest of his body loose, hair blowing crazy, hundreds of feet up above the Hudson, the grossest most infectious part of this river, but none of that matters since he'd die before landing anyway, his back would break during the fall.

I just stand there and watch him, too scared to move. Cars go by, but in the dark no one notices.

"Do it or I'll let go," he says.

"What the fuck?"

"Don't fuck with this, Logan. Look at me. I'm gone. I'm letting go, I'm a goner, I'm gone goodbye never gonna see me again. Do it."

What I think is, this guy doesn't really have a lot to lose, with all the people in the world who hate him. So I do what the fucker tells me to do.

"All right, Jesus. All right."

My hands get all clammy and my legs tremble like two wobbly sticks. I pretend it's nothing. I pretend it's just one of those monkey bars at the jungle gym. I climb over the rail, one leg at a time. My body gets all hot and hollow feeling and I clutch on and the metal burns my hands. I look down and it's like hundreds of feet. This is what I think. I think family is a terrible thing that happens to you. And if things were fair, like if they made sense, I'd let this motherfucker go. But I climb over and hold onto the steel. I stand next to my brother like that, my feet clutching the rail, trembling. When you're holding on to your life on the rail of the George Washington Bridge pedestrian path, something happens to you. First of all, you go nuts. I don't know what it is, if it's the weight of gravity at your back, or the fact that you are so close to death, or the fact that you know what you're doing falls outside of normal behavior, but in the chance of falling, in the heart pumping scared clammy world spinning dizziness you feel, with the wind in your face and pushing you, there is this space. This letting go of all the things in the world you know and are used to. And that's what's crazy. You don't scramble. You just kind of breathe. My brother and I. This doesn't last very long at all. It's really just split seconds that I'm up here with my back towards the river, my crazy brother by my side. It feels like eight hundred thousand years, like there's no point in even counting. My brother always feels this way. For me, it's like feeling the world for the first time.

Teddy hops over the rail to the sidewalk, grabs onto me, and pulls me up to safety. He hugs me real tight, wraps me inside of his hug until it hurts. He takes his thumbs and presses them into my face.

"You really thought I was going to let go, huh? You think I'm nuts, don't you?"

"I'm going home."

"It's for your own good, though. Things are too easy for you at home. You're going to have a shock when you get out into the real world. It's full of assholes like me."

"You could have died, you fucking jackass."

"Logan, you love me," he says. "Why don't you just admit it?"

We walk. It's been such a long time since I've cried. I hold the tears in my throat. I try and swallow the lump and I cough and Teddy asks me what time I was supposed to be home, and I shrug my shoulders and he asks me what's wrong and thank God for the dark and I start bawling in the middle of the suburban street, blurry with my tears.

"Jesus Christ," is all Teddy says. He holds my hand, squeezes once, and lets go. I think for a second to tell him not to tell anyone. But who's there to tell?

We walk all the way home and stop at the driveway. One light in the house is on. We see my mother in the kitchen. Teddy looks at her, then down at the gravel. He inches the tip of his shoe into the driveway, then pulls back, like it's electric or something. He looks at the house again.

"She's up late," he says. "The woman's a vampire."

"She just thinks a lot," I say.

"Yeah. She thinks. She just thinks and thinks."

"You want to come want to come in for a second," I ask him. "There's tons of food. Pie and cheese and pork chops and stuff. We could be quiet."

"Nah, I go to go," he says. "You go inside an do what your mother says, okay?"

"Okay," I say.

When I come inside, Mom is sitting at the kitchen table, having tea and painting with watercolors. It's late, probably close to three. I go straight to the bathroom to wash my face.

"Where have you been?" she says. Not too harsh or anything.

"Just out."

"You should leave a note next time."

"I was just out with some friends, Mom."

"Derrick wasn't invited?"

"He goes to sleep too early."

"Early to bed's a good habit."

"What are you doing up, are you okay?"

"I'm fine."

"This one looks nice," I say, meaning the painting.

"Thanks, Logan."

My mom could have been a famous painter, I think.

I give her a kiss on the cheek, and I start to go upstairs to her bed. On my way up, I stay in the hall outside the kitchen to look at all her paintings. She has a thing for moons and beaches and old bridges in Italy. That's all her paintings are about. One after another, all lined up in rows. Then comes that photo of my grandfather. He doesn't look anything like my dad, none of my dad's dark coloring or anything, but then if you look hard, look in between his eyes, at his nose, at his eyelashes, you can totally tell they're related.

"Mom, can I ask you something?"

"What?"

"Why does Dad keep that robe in the closet?"

"Why don't you ask him?

"He doesn't talk about it."

"I think he doesn't know what to do with it."

"He could just throw it away."

"Maybe he thinks it's important."

"It's a strange kind of a thing to hang on to."

"I know it is."

"Would you get rid of it?"

"I don't know."

"Why don't you tell him to get rid of it?"

"I'm not here to tell people what to do. Maybe someday he'll have use for it in the classroom or something."

"He's a freak," I say.

"That's true," she says smiling, and I go upstairs. I almost ask, speaking of freaks, why she always walks around in the dark in the backyard saying things, but I decide not to, since she's painting now and seems so relaxed and happy.

"What are you writing?" Derrick asks, startling me because I thought he was asleep. He is lying on his bed, and I don't know how long he's been staring at me. His head is in his hands.

"Nothing," I say.

"What nothing? Every night I wake up and you're writing.

You think I'm asleep, but I hear the stupid pen scratching. Anyone can hear you. What are you writing?"

"It's nothing special," I say.

"Is it homework?"

"No, it's nothing."

"What, are you like some stupid girl writing in your diary?"

"It's not a diary."

"Are you writing shit about me?'

"It's just words."

"Words, huh? Let me see."

"Go back to bed."

"I'm in bed."

"Fall asleep, then, jackass."

"I can't sleep."

"What do you mean you can't sleep—you're always asleep."

"But what are you writing about?'

"I told you, it's just words."

He comes over to my bed and rips the black book out of my hands. I try to snatch it back but he holds it up, standing on the bed, and it's out of my reach. He flips through the pages and pages of words.

"These are just words," he says.

"Told you."

"It doesn't make any sense."

"So?"

"So? What do you mean? So you're a fucking weirdo."

"Up yours."

He throws the book at my headboard and climbs back into his own bed. He turns over and pulls the covers over his head. I pick up the book and start where I left off, I keep writing down words, they keep coming, and I feel like I can't catch up. I look down at the paper to see what I have. What I have looks like this:

Tomorrow tackle dead fish boot hurt night cow sung fly teapot eleven jingle forget stone shrine tile road cry wet stuck belt sweat hair tooth wood rot feast river dynamite over again leap nightmare sand boat statue puppet dog stone crash bread tangle burnt fever spasm crush ten lick sprain strawberry fuck glove bat monster hungry city slaughter maggot ice cloud music red magnet forever smooth care bleach sweatshirt neck spice trash coffee toothpaste air skateboard jacket.

And it goes on like that for pages.

"But why are you writing words?" he asks.

I ignore him. I turn my head towards the window. I swear at night I have super power hearing. I can hear things a million miles away. Planes flying, dogs barking, my mom pacing outside, my dad sipping water in the next room, the refrigerator, the electricity running through the walls, I swear, even from upstairs, I can hear the fireflies lighting up and fading in the dark backyard. The whole world is such a quiet damn place and it makes me hear. I write the word quiet down in the book. Then I start writing down all the things in the world that are quiet the way I always do with my lists. I start writing so fast, my pen makes this frantic scratching noise on the paper, and part of me knows it might be annoying, might keep my twin brother awake, but right now I can't stop, I just keep going.

The Sentimental Thieves

My house is robbed every day for a week. Every day, the thieves come in through a different window and take objects of absolutely no value. This is what they could have taken: my electric guitar, my VCR, my leather jacket, some very expensive kitchen knives, a silver watch that belongs to my older brother. But this is what they did take, in chronological order. Monday: torn up boots; Tuesday: a typewriter with a few missing keys; Wednesday: an ugly dress I've never worn; Thursday: some crusty yellow books on sailing; and Friday: a box full of random photos.

What low-life thieves of St. Paul, Minnesota could possibly need with a stranger's photographs, with any of these items, I have no idea. And yet, they specifically take them. They scrounge through my closets, open up trunks, forage through bookshelves. And here's what's strange: every day they leave my house immaculate. When

I come home, I spend hours trying to put my house back into the state it was in when I left it. I unmake the bed, scatter clothes everywhere, open up cabinets, fill the sink up with dirty dishes, and throw papers, envelopes, and sneakers on the floor where they belong.

I don't call the cops. Why bother the cops for a pair of black boots, for some crusty old books on sailing?

My junkie big brother lives on the other side of town and I call him instead. He isn't home. Or he is home, shooting up, and he doesn't pick up the phone. On his machine, I tell him about the burglary. About the things the thieves took and the things they left behind. I don't expect him to, but he calls back when I'm out and leaves a message. My brother's got polyps on his vocal chords from singing and smoking. He sounds like he just woke up from two weeks of sleep.

"That's weird," is all he says and he hangs up. He calls back ten minutes later.

"I need the silver watch they didn't take," he says. "Call me when you get this."

Friday night I can't sleep and decide to call the cops. Who knows what these thieves are looking for? And what if they're dangerous with dangerous plans? What kind of sociopaths would steal an ugly dress and a broken typewriter?

The cop walks in on Saturday morning. He's short and reminds me of my grandfather. If my grandfather had been nice. He takes one look at my apartment, at the mess, looks at me solemnly, and puts his hand on my shoulder.

"Did they do this?" he asks.

"No," I say. And I explain the peculiar habits of my tidy thieves.

He takes notes. He paces through my apartment, looking at all my things. He is very careful not to step on all the papers and clothes on the floor.

"Do you have any enemies?" he asks.

If I have any enemies, I don't know who they are. The man at the post office certainly hates me. He doesn't like the way I wrap my packages, and how I always ask for tape. I used to hate my parents, but now I think they're the only human beings alive. I have some ex-girlfriends but they all live in Brooklyn now, and probably have better looking enemies.

"Not really. Not that I can think of," I say.

He hands me a police report to fill out, even though I know I won't.

"Thank you for calling," he says. "I will tell your neighbors. And maybe you should put bars on these windows."

But I could never live in a house with bar-covered windows.

On Sunday, my brother and I meet at a coffee shop for lunch. It's been forever since I've seen him, and when his big red truck pulls into the parking lot, I feel a wave of nervousness. I take the watch from my pocket and put it on the table. It's old and dirty, but worth something.

We eat our sandwiches in silence. My brother barely touches his. He takes small bites and chews each mouthful slowly. He's gotten skinny, I've decided. His arms are covered in red marks and his face is the color of ash. How did he get like this, I wonder. There was a time when I thought he was the only happy person in the world. Now I look at him and wonder how a man can live to be thirty and make nothing of his life.

"I don't know why they're doing this," I say. "What do these people want from me?"

"Maybe they own a thrift store," he says. "Maybe people have stopped giving things away and there's a shortage of junk. Maybe they're kids on a treasure hunt. Maybe they're apprentice thieves who aren't shady enough to steal important things."

"The strange thing is, I can't stop thinking about the things they took away," I say. "I never thought about those things before. But even the books on sailing. Those were Dad's books. I could have had them around a little while. And what about the cleaning thing? Why are they picking up after me?"

My brother shrugs his shoulders. He looks down at the un-eaten sandwich and puts his face in his hands.

"I'm having some trouble," he finally says, and when he looks up, I can see tears in his eyes.

When he leaves, he takes the watch, and for a second, I miss it. It was never really his watch. I know he'd forgotten about it until I mentioned it. It once belonged to my favorite uncle and now my big brother will pawn it for drugs.

At night, I have dreams about thieves. I dream about a man with no face wearing the dress and the boots, reading about sailing. I dream about a woman typing letters on the broken type-writer, going through my photographs. I wake up in the middle of the night and think about the photos. They are mostly photos of friends—friends whose faces I will now certainly forget. They are also photos from trips across the country, when I was younger and my life was just starting.

And I can't stop thinking about the boots. The boots I wore every day of my twenties. They were so big and so black, the most perfect boots.

And that horrible dress. I never wore it. But it would have been a good costume. With the boots, it might have looked okay.

And the typewriter. It was so broken. It was just like the person I was when I bought it: cheap and full of promises.

And of course, the books on sailing. I could have been a sailor. One night in the future, bored of reading novels, I could have picked up a crusty yellow book on sailing, which might have inspired me to save up for a boat, which would have forced me to get a real job, which would have relieved me of debt, which would have changed my life completely.

I hear noises from downstairs, and I know it's the thieves. I pull the covers over my head and listen. I hear fumbling in the kitchen, the clattering of plates, the moving around of furniture. I listen. I clutch on to the blankets, afraid of what they would do to me if they saw that I was home, and I hold my breath to make less noise, and I wish I'd taken the cop's advice about the bars, wish I'd installed an alarm. I'm afraid of the things they might take this time, things that might leave more holes.

I hear the door slam shut.

When I wake up the next morning, my house is clean. My electric guitar, my VCR, the leather jacket, and the knives are gone. Outside on the porch are the useless things: the black boots, the old typewriter, the ugly dress, the crusty books, the box of photos, and the silver watch, fixed, ticking, shining in the light.

Prayer

Let me ride my bike to heaven. I've got new reflectors. The road's smooth, all fixed up for the club of upward trekkers. I've got a bag of bananas. I've got a bell makes you know I'm coming. The front basket's full of books. Old ones I forgot to read. Now I have time. All there's left. All sewn together on the spines. All once misplaced, now found. Notes in the margins. Underline every word reminds me of her. The beach ahead, not five miles. I'm going with my jacket that turns into a cape. If you fall, you fly. I've got new shoes with no laces, so they won't get caught in the spokes. My socks match. The bike's new. I won't let that bastard steal it. I'll say bastard then bastard son of a bitch no you won't steal my bike, you little Christ. Whatever's on the road, if it breathes, ride it. If a kid comes running out of the water, just let me go.

Of Dogs and Dreams

But the sad part, my father said. *The part that ruined me was how her dreams stunk. They reeked like street dogs, for dogs ran through her dreams. In the middle of the night, she often whispered those dreams in my ear. How they crawled to her wearing crowns. I suppose they were kings. Those dogs took her down on the stairs, in the hallway, in the basement, their pink cocks knobbed and hungry, a house full of dogs, their teeth ripped through her dress. And the unruly tongues of those dogs, she told me how they flapped and dripped for her sex. Like a pig, she let them have her, her legs splayed open, her nipples falling out, she fed them. And I couldn't sleep with the smell of those dreams. They entered mine. And not clean dogs, either. Dogs with maggots dripping from their nostrils. Dogs that had lived in garbage cans, whose mouths had sucked the bones of raw chickens, that had eaten the feces from each other's asses, that had sniffed the sexes of dead bitches. Summer time dogs with no homes, no water, heaving, blood of discarded meat rotted in the spaces between their teeth. Mouths like that covered her. Their cocks slipped into her one by one, and I smelled her dreams of their collective cum.*

The room where my mother lay was full of flowers. Everyone we knew had sent them. The cards hung by the window on a string. My wife clutched my hand. She looked at me for answers. I shook my head slowly. My father looked out the window at the street as he spoke and never faced us, never turned to the bed with the sheet pulled over her body. We watched the back of his bald pink head. He played with a toothpick in his right hand, moved it as though he were drawing small circles in the air with a pen.

I'm sure you kids would love for me to tell you the story of love, how it will go on and on so steadily, so solemnly but steadily. How wonderful it will be. The houses you will build. The children you will grow and tend to like gardens. Until the dogs come into the delicate head of your bride and you suffocate in the home you built with your hands. And life is long, he said, almost whispering. *It is long and so unbearably long. There is no recess, no break from the smell of it, never, not even when you sleep, not even for a moment.*

Swim With Horses

That was the winter of the horse thief, and so how do you expect me to forget it?

He was some kid down in the dumps. Lived on the West Side with his parents. Good family, good teeth, good jeans, good school, good prospects, good accumulator of good lovers, everything good except his life was total garbage. How else could we explain that event away? What will take the blame for that last misstep in judgment, for that spontaneous lapse in reason, for the extended hallucination that led him to the horse stables in Central Park to free two miserable animals, to unhook them from their hinges, this in broad daylight, and then down 8th Avenue riding one horse, trailing another? Through traffic, through the rigid population of the West 50's, in its buzzing Midtown splendor, in its early evening sidewalk chaos, in the grumbling constipated pedestrian packed streets, the taxis and the heavy coated women and the business men and the theater fags and the pizza delivery bicycles and the little dogs, this kid riding a stolen horse, riding it like the Lone Ranger through the desert, like Billy The Kid through the prairie, but through the concrete, undeterred by the Broadway lights, by the oncoming traffic, by the accumulating crowd of shocked and pissed-off bystanders, by the Citizens for Central Park Horse Rides, wearing their best masks of selfless concern. Galloping on that horse with abandon, this kid, some might even say with ecstatic delight, headed undistracted for the East River, jumping over fire hydrants and manholes, over a bunch of stoned lazing truant Central Park girls.

And why horses? And how old was this kid anyway? What was his name? For the purposes of this story, let's say his name was Steve. Steve had always wanted to be a horse. He didn't want to be Alec, the boy in *The Black Stallion* whose goodness and love for his horse overcame the rigid cruelty of the adult world. No, Steve wanted to be the stallion. All sorts of psychosexual subtexts may be inferred from this equestrian desire and even from the mere mention of horses in this or any story. Let us detach ourselves from any preconceived notions we have of the idea of horses, of their conscious and unconscious role in the amalgamated mythologies of our society, of our mastery of them, of their power over us, of the muscle bound beast between the rider's legs, and the requisite thrusting motion embedded in this image. Those are just dreams. Yours. Keep them to yourself. This really happened. It was in the world. The Post covered it. I read it. And so when I tell you this story do not try to understand its meaning. Understand instead the inherent physical problems involved in two horses galloping recklessly through the city. Imagine the risk of physical injury both for the rider and the watchers. Imagine how awkward it would be to ride a horse through the city while trailing a horse.

And not two stallions either. More like the horses that end up in Central Park. Going around the skating rink. From the rink to the Sheep Meadow. From the Sheep Meadow to the Alice in Wonderland Statue. You know, the life of a Central Park Horse. Clop clop clop. Plop plop plop. And the taxis speed around you and the cameras go click. It's bad in the winter and worse in the summer. The fall is the only good time to be alive. In the Spring, you just wish someone would hang you, turn you into glue. With all the lovers shtupping in the bushes, you wish you were born glue.

Go down now to the East River where he leapt.

He wasn't a kid really. He was actually almost thirty. He was a grown man, Steve. Some would argue his best years were already over. He'd had lovers. And they'd turned his life to the garbage it was as he sank. And don't be cute with the horses and the water and the young man trying to save them. Or trying to save himself in this moment, the delight now disappearing from his face. Into the winter water, the East River in winter, the East River ferocious and brown and holding the waste of Brooklyn, Queens, the Bronx, and Manhattan, the hypothermia coming into his nostrils, into his lungs, in his finger tips, in his toes, his chest contracting, coming up for air, and down again and air again, his good jeans weighing down now in frozen water, and then it was night, the bridges above the bridges and barges and Queens rusted in the distance somewhere far off, but all of this unseen. Just pulling the mammoth animals, pulling their manes, these two horses. One of them kicking, the other one, resigned. One kicking full force, all fours and the head bucking, a ton of beast gone mad, the other, dead and giving its entire weight into the water.

And the kid's family was there, on the other side of the East River. Just watching him.

Probably laughing. His sister and his father, just laughing. Nobody tried to jump in, call the Department of Parks and Rivers, call the Police, the ambulance, the search and rescue, the Coastguard, call the fucking mayor's office, nobody picked up the phone, made a phone call just watched him trying to swim these two horses, these two fat merry-go-round horses through that water, just watched and laughed, or it seemed like it, like they were laughing.

Song of Winter

Gino Ronconni was my father and he lost his job when I was thirteen. He did not look for a new one. He began to make our lunches. At seven in the morning, wearing an apron, his flannel shirt open underneath. We'd always made our own lunches or bought them at school. Now my father made them. Now he baked the bread himself. As I brushed my teeth one morning, I could smell the yeast. It was sour and made me sick, the way it filled the house. I don't think he slept much at night or even took a bath. He sat at the kitchen table until it was time to bake the bread.

My mother taught a ballet class and had a weeping-bathing habit. When I asked Ronconni why she cried so much, he said it was the tearwater bath.

"The tearwater bath, Louis, it's good for the skin. Your mother's vain. What she wouldn't do for beauty. But every one grows old. Salt or none. You'll see, you too. One day you'll end up fat or lose control of your bladder. Lines will appear under your eyes and everyone will see how many years you've lived and how hard you've lived them. It happens to the best and worst and everyone in the middle. There's nothing to do about it. We all end up ugly and dead. But still your mother cries that way to fill the tub."

He slapped some butter on the bread and put the sandwiches in a brown bag. He drank his coffee slowly. The leaves outside were dead. He had nothing to do all day but rake them.

"The leaves," he said. "The leaves. If you had an ounce of muscle on that skinny rail of yours, you'd have risen this morning and raked the leaves. But did he? No he didn't. He did NOT. What does he do? He waits for the world to make his lunch so that he can trot to school. School. Does it matter we send him there? Does he learn a goddamn thing? Or does he stare out the window like an imbecile and fail every test he takes?"

He went outside and stood on the porch, looking at the street and the front steps full of leaves. I took a drag of the cigarette he'd left burning in the ashtray. I coughed out the smoke and gathered my homework to go to school.

"And another thing," he said, coming back into the house. "Another thing…"

But I guess he'd forgotten what it was because all he did was sit down with his head in his hands. He was not a crier like my mother. He was a sitter-smoker.

"Go to school, for Christ's sake," he finally said, and my brother and I took our sandwich bags and walked out the front door.

My little brother wanted a lunchbox. We kept buying the

brown bags that the rain would soak and tear to bits. He had dreams about that lunchbox. Every day, the lunchbox, the lunchbox.

"Shut up about the lunchbox, Mikey, just shut up about it."

"I want a lunchbox. I want the one with Star Wars…"

"Just shut up about the lunchbox. What's the difference? You still get the same lunch."

"I don't like the lunch."

"What's the difference? So you don't like it, just don't eat it."

"I hate it."

"Tough tits."

He was right, though. The lunch was always lousy. The lunch was that bread my father insisted on baking with just a slap of butter on it, no jam or peanut butter or anything. Sometimes a pickle or yogurt and a handful of raisins. No fruit leather or string cheese.

"It's gross. I hate it."

"Oh who cares, just shut up. Some kids don't have anything to eat, how would you like that, Mikey, how would you like to have nothing, how would you like to be one of those kids who rides the short bus and has to eat mashed up corn? Anyway, what's the difference? With a lunchbox or without one, you still get the same lunch."

"But why can't I…"

"Just shut up, Mikey. Pick up your coat, for God's sake. Look at the way it's trailing behind you."

"But…"

"Don't talk to me."

"Why not?"

"I'm trying to think."

"What are you thinking about?"

"Nothing."

"Tell me."

"You wouldn't understand."

"Why not?"

"Don't walk so close to me. Pretend you don't know me."

"Everyone knows I know you."

"Pretend you don't."

He walked right behind me for about five minutes, kicking stones and trash, sometimes stepping on the back of my heel. Talking to himself. He walked up to my side and I took his hand. It was cold and small. He wore one of my father's old raincoats that trailed behind him in the dirt, stupidly long sleeves, and a hard rain hat, the kind mailmen wear. He's stolen it from the mailman.

"You should give that hat back."

" I don't know where he lives."

At school he ate his butter sandwich by himself while the other kids played in the tunnel slide. I saw him at my recess when I stood with the older kids.

"Hey Ronconni, isn't that your little brother over there"

"Yeah, that's him."

"What's he doing?"

"I don't know."

"Is he talking to himself?"

"I don't know."

"Well, what the hell's wrong with him?"

"Nothing's wrong with him, what do you mean?"

"I mean, look at him."

I looked at him. He was talking to himself, throwing crumbs at the pigeons with that hat on.

"What kind of hat is that anyway?"

"It's a mailman's hat."

Ronconni hadn't raked the leaves. He hadn't moved all day. He was sitting in the same position, smoking. The ashtray overflowed with cigarette butts and there were broken cigarettes in piles all over the kitchen table. My father sat in the smoke, in a daze. He had not changed his clothes. He still wore the apron. Everything was the same as the morning, except for the cigarettes and it was almost dark. The sky was pink. Winter would be here soon. I needed winter so bad. I needed snow. I wanted to wake up and have the whole town covered in it. I wanted to lie down in it, go to sleep there. Anything but fall. Fall was the worst. Fall came with everything bad. School and leaves and bad news. The three of us waited for my mother to come home. It was quiet. We could hear the neighbors, home from work, their car doors slamming shut.

Mikey and I started dinner. He still wore the hat. He set the table and I put the water on the stove for pasta. Ronconni sat there without moving.

"Well, there's nothing to do," he said. "There's nothing in the world to do but wait."

It was the first thing anyone said all night.

"Let me tell you a story about the house that was eaten by leaves," he said. "Listen carefully, this is very important. You too, Louis."

Mikey sat down at the table and listened. His eyes lit up. He set the hat on the table.

"There was a house not too far from here…there was a house not too far from here. A house like this one. An empty house… empty except for a warlock. What do you think, Mikey? Do you think he ever raked the leaves?"

"No!"

"Do you think he ever brushed his teeth?"

"No!"

"Do you think his teeth were mossy and the house was mossy and the piles of leaves grew taller than the windows?"

"Yes!"

"Did he have warts on his forehead? Scarlet and the size of radishes?"

"Yes!"

"Do you think flames came out of his nostrils? Did the leaves catch fire? Did the whole house burn down?"

I heard my mother running her bath in the middle of the night. I went to the hallway to listen to the water run into the tub. Ronconni was asleep downstairs in the kitchen on a pile of our coats. He had a beard now, and I swear if it weren't for the bread every morning I'd be able to smell his sweat from all the way up in my room. No wonder she didn't want him. He'd turned into a hairy beast. But which was first? Was my father ever easy to look at? I couldn't remember. Was she the one who made him that way? Why did you make him ugly, Mom? What did he ever do to you, Mom? It would kill you to be happy? How would you like to be one of those people who doesn't have anyone, who has to spend the night alone? Can't you see him? How would you like to lose your job? I couldn't remember when he worked. It was only months before, but

I couldn't remember his face then, or what his voice sounded like. The water stopped running and I heard her climb in. I imagined her in the tub. Her black hair in the bun. Her torn ballet feet resting on the edge. The tears would come soon. Hers and mine.

"Mom," I said. I walked into the bathroom.

"Louis," she said. The water had drained. She didn't cover herself. "My little Louis."

She was beautiful. Even with her eyes wet, any idiot could she see was beautiful.

"Where did you go?"

"I just need some time to walk, baby. There's nothing wrong with walking, is there? I have dances in my head and I need to walk them out, think about them alone. Everybody needs to be alone sometimes, right? Oh, baby."

I tried to hold them back but they came out of my eyes.

"How's Mikey?"

"Fine."

But he wasn't. Anyone could see the kid was off. I waited for him to do something every day. I had a dream he burned down the house. He burned down the school. He burned down the dance studio. He burned down the town. Why would you do a thing like that? I asked him in my dreams. Why would you burn things? He stood on the mountains of ash where the town had been and shrugged his shoulders. He laughed. *I don't know,* he said. *I did it because I felt like it. I can do whatever I want.*

My mother reached her hand towards my face, but she didn't lift herself from the tub and she didn't touch me. She smiled.

"You are my men," she said.

"The warlock had no friends," Ronconni said the next night at dinner, out of nowhere. We ate beans and corn. He spoke slowly, very carefully bringing the spoon of corn and beans to his mouth, like a patient in a hospital bed. The food stuck to his teeth as he spoke.

"He only had a very skinny, very ugly dog that he chained outside to his fence. The dog sang at night. Do you know what song? The song of winter. You could hear that awful song deep in the night. The warlock stole chickens from the farm next door and fed his dog the chicken bones. Worms lived in the warlock's hair. Blue blood and fat from the uncooked chickens stuck to his beard. The dead chicken fat rotted on his face. His teeth stunk. His gums bled. He had a metal comb that he kept in a box, but he never used it. He only took the comb out of the box once in a while and ran it along his hand."

He held Mikey's hand and pressed his long nails into it his palm. Mikey let him, his eyes huge.

"Like this," he said. "He pressed those comb teeth into his hand so hard, there were holes in his skin. No one loved him. No one could love a man like that. Not even you could love him."

He looked at Mikey's hand and dropped it.

"Did the warlock smoke?" Mikey asked.

"No. He didn't." Ronconni put out his cigarette. "Go to bed."

The man my mother slept with now didn't look like anyone I'd ever met. He was tall with a sharp pointed face. I saw them together one night. I stood outside the County Discount across the street from the studio. The light was on and I saw them through the glass doors. Anyone could see them. The ballerina girls had left. My mother and the man stood close together. He wore a long black coat and my mother wore her leotard. She fell into his chest. They kissed. I watched for a moment, their faces pressed together. The lights went off. I smoked, walking home.

"A warlock who's lost his powers is just a man. And what is a man without a horse? A man without a horse is just a dog. And what do you think he thought about all alone at night? That's the story no one tells. You don't learn it at school. What happens to a man like that? Those gone from him forever powers, his cheeks punctured all over, and his tongue, torn away. Everything goes bad like meat," my father said. "The whole world turns blue. What a terrible thing. To love when you are old and ugly when you have no magic and you cannot speak with your ruined tongue. I used to dream of boats and women the way young men do. And I don't have anything anymore. I don't even remember my dreams. Or the last time I really slept."

Mikey lit my father's cigarette. He inhaled, staring past his son, his eyes glazed in sadness.

"Let me see your tongue," he said to Mikey.

My brother stuck it out. "That's good," Ronconni, said. "That's a good meaty tongue. We'll cut it out and eat it if we get hungry."

I sat on the edge of the toilet as my mother bathed.

"Who is he?" I ask her quietly.

"Who is who?"

"Who is he? What's his name? Where did he come from?"

She sat up in the tub.

"I'm very tired, Louis. Why don't you eat something? Where's your brother?"

"How old is he? Is he young?"

"Make me some tea, baby. Put the water on for me. I don't feel like going down there."

We heard my father drag chairs across the kitchen floor.

"And his hands," I asked. "What does it feel like when they touch you?"

"Louis."

She did not look at me.

"Tell me what it feels like," I said.

"Your father makes me insane. But he is still your father..."

"Tell me what he feels like."

She turned the faucet off. She pulled one foot out of the water, placed the bottom of it against the tile of the wall. Her large wet toes curled into the grout. She kept them curled. She closed her eyes and put her fingers on her neck.

"Very soft," she whispered. "Very slow."

Ronconni moved slowly through the kitchen, doing things at the table. He picked up a cup, put it in the sink. He took a dish from the stove, put it on the counter. He took the teapot off the stove and placed it on the table. I followed him around the kitchen, putting things back from where he'd moved them, but he waved me away, grumbling under his breath.

I tried to help him find a job, looked at ads in the newspaper. What about carpentry? I asked him. This company's looking for carpenters. You're good at that, Dad, you're good with your hands. You could move furniture. You could work at the shoe store, there was a sign, I saw this sign, it would be no big deal, if you just work there, maybe not full-time, maybe part-time. Part-time there, part-time somewhere else. You could be a fireman, Dad. They're always looking. You're strong, Dad. You're smart, Dad. You could do it, Dad. They say you need to know how to type. You can type, Dad. I've seen you type. He stopped his lectures in the morning. He stopped going on about the leaves. He only told my brother stories.

Now the warlock had a garden of dead horses. The bodies of dead horses stank up the town. The air in the town was thick with flies, the way my father described it. But I didn't think about the flies or the horses or how their deadness made everyone gag on hot summer nights and the warlock, lonely in his shack. I only thought of my mother in the bath, the secret she told me, and the soft slow fucking of the tall young man. I imagined parts of him, his skin, his chest, flashes of his cock, never his face, never my mother as she took him.

Ronconni was right. There was no point in sending me to school. I tried to read but I didn't care about any of the stories. All the stories seemed like lies. They were all about people from a long time ago. And even if they were true, probably the people were all dead by now, so who cared. I tried to do the math problems, but the numbers spun around on the page. Pay attention, Louis. Stop daydreaming. Focus, Louis. This is important. This is fractions, Louis. We've been over all of this, this is easy stuff.

I couldn't sleep. I spent the nights waiting for my mother and she came home later and later. I kept thinking of Mikey, how he was just about to do it. He was going to do it, just snap. Would we be in the house? Every sound I heard, my father stirring downstairs, my mother in her bath, the windows rattling in the night, I thought it was maybe Mikey up to something. I checked on him one night, but he was in bed. I sat on his bed and watched him sleep. He was tiny in the bed. Calm down, Louis, I said to myself. Everything is going to be fine. He's just a little weird, that's all. What's wrong with being weird? What's so wrong with that? You think you're so normal? If you're so normal, why are you talking to yourself? If you're so normal, why can't you sleep? In the middle of the night, I prayed for snow. Snow would do it. They would cancel school, I'd get my Dad to go outside. Take us on the toboggan down hills. That's what he needed, just to have some fun. But it was like he was trapped in the kitchen, just watching everything fall.

I visited my mother once more in the bathtub late at night.

"You didn't rake the leaves again this morning, Louis."

Wasn't it time for secrets?

"How many times does your father tell you every day to rake the leaves? But you don't do it. They just get worse and worse."

She sponged her face.

"And I'd like you to take care of your brother more. Help out with errands, things like that. We won't have you sleeping in on Saturdays. School called. You're failing."

"I'm done with school."

"Go rake the leaves."

"It's the middle of the night."

"Do it now."

She pulled the shower curtain forward.

I stood for a moment in the bathroom. I looked at myself in the mirror above the sink. I turned my head to the side. My eyes had pillows under them. Every one in the house was tired. I had already lived too many years and now my eyes were showing it.

"You shouldn't be in here," my mother said.

The trees in our town kept growing leaves. Every time you thought, that is the last leaf from the last tree, more leaves would fall. They'd clog up the gutters and the drains. Dogs would piss on them, and you'd have piles of yellow and brown mush. There was a problem with fires at night. That's why I always had those fire dreams. Fuck these leaves. I raked the yard into piles. I remembered playing in them as a little kid. Lying down in the dirt smell of them. Getting wet covered in them. I thought of all of that in the yard in the dark, doing the task my mother had told me to do, raking, just because she'd told me to do it. I don't know why after all that work I'd do a thing like this, but I put down the rake and ran into the piles. I ruined them. Completely covered, I listened under them, in the middle of the night, the quiet crunch every time I breathed. I thought if I died out here. If I just fell asleep and died.

"What are you doing out here?" Mikey asked.

He stood next to the pile of leaves in his pajamas and boots and oversized raincoat. He fell down on the leaves next to me.

"I'm building a house," I said.

"Why are you building a house?"

"It's for the warlock's dog. He needs a house of his own."

"Let me help you."

"Go find me some sticks," I said.

We heard glass breaking from inside the house. My mother yelled and something else broke. She yelled again. More breaking. She screamed. What came next happened slowly. The backdoor creaked open. My father crawled out of the doorway on his knees. He was naked. Mikey looked at me as though I would know what to do. I looked at the thing before us. His hair was disheveled. His chin had been cut and it bled. I thought: and now Ronconni will cry. But he did not cry. He did something worse. He sang. His voice was enormous and faint all at once. Like an opera, but the quiet part. He barely moved his lips as the words came out, but when they did I felt his voice moving the insides of my stomach.

> *A home to rest*
> *My burning chest…*

I thought the song would never end. It did not seem like he knew we were watching him, although anyone could see us with the light from the back porch. My mother threw his clothes out the bedroom window. His shirts and socks and pants and shoes came falling on the leaves. He scuttled on his knees to gather them. Mikey began to help him pick up the clothes, but I held him back. The song continued:

> *The teeth of winter*
> *Will cut my bones*
> *Will crush my lungs*
> *Will freeze my tears*
> *To stones.*

He howled the last note. He continued to crawl around the garden to the other side of the house, and then, I guess, down the street, and after that, who knows where he went. He stayed away for weeks. What happened while he was gone? I don't remember what it was like without him. There was school, there were leaves, there were my mother's late night baths. Mikey still wore the hat and still talked about the lunchbox.

"Did I ever tell you why your mother dances, Louis?"

Ronconni drank is coffee in the kitchen. He was about to leave for his new job at the factory. They had finally bought Mikey a Star Wars lunchbox and I made a ham sandwich for him while my father talked about my mother.

He laughed. "Because she can't sit still. It's a strange disease she has. If she sits still, she dies. That's why she moves around that way. It's always been like that, ever since I've known her. She'll be like that when she's a thousand years old. Ridiculous, I know. Heheheheh."

He stopped laughing and stared at something outside, but I couldn't tell what he was looking at. He put on his coat and wrapped a scarf around his neck. I saw a little sadness in his eyes, but it passed quickly. I looked outside. It was snowing little flutters.

"Except of course when she's taking a bath," he said. "When she's taking a bath, she's fine. She can sit for hours and hours in that bath of hers, soaking away. Once she gets out of water, it's off to dancing. Heheheheh."

He left.

Late that night, I lay in my bed, listening to the water fill the tub. My mother and Ronconni slept together again and he stopped spending entire days in the kitchen. Winter was finally here. Thank God, I thought. They had predicted snow every day for the entire week. They would cancel school and we would go out on the toboggan. But I wasn't going to mind school anyway. No, not anymore. From now on, I thought. From now on, life would be different. I was going to start studying. I'd be the smartest kid at school. There he goes, that's him. That's Louis. The smartest kid who ever went here. You should see how fast he solves math problems. He's a reader too. A great reader of books. I heard once he saved his mother from a burning house. He once fought a warlock who came after the whole family in the middle of the night. I hear he's a prince. His mother is a queen. His father is the strongest man alive. His little brother...

"Louis?"

Mikey walked into my room.

"What's wrong?"

"I feel weird."

"What is it?"

"Something's wrong with my ribs."

"What's wrong with them?"

"My ribs are frozen. They're icicles. They turned into icicles in my chest."

He came close to my bed. I touched his chest. He was freezing. The house was freezing.

"Come sleep by me," I said.

American Memoir

I was born on the interstate, one eye sewn shut, the other over-flowing.

"Crocodile tears," Dad said to Mom from the front seat. Mom was half-mute. She couldn't speak but sang like the birds. Mean ones. Not in words but in twittering notes. I came out slick and easy covered in mud and swore I'd never go back.

I did. The night I turned twelve. "All promises are broken," I announced in her bedroom. She opened herself to me. "Every-thing gold is blue again." Dad slept next to us, a deafening snorer. Needless to say we did not get a wink.

Nor did we dream. Instead I spent the night tearing at her nightgown, sweating under sheets. She was wet between her legs like on the day I was born. I pushed myself inside of her. I felt underwater. At the bottom of a lukewarm cup of tea. "Get out of that cunt!" I heard Dad shout himself awake. "Come back to me, or I swear to you I'll die." He was an ornery king—short, fat and full of smoke. A face like the ass of a pig. You would have laughed. He loved to fight. It was so easy to kill him.

Something to Do

Self, I say to myself. What is going on with you? For two nights now, you haven't slept. Every morning this week you've had The Earlies. Not the good kind of early where you drink orange juice and read the paper and start your day before the world. The bad early, where you wake up too early and it's dark in the city and it's silent and you wish more than life you could fall back asleep and downtown is staring at you through the window with its mean red lights and there is no sound except the I-80 and the broken heater. It's been going on too long now. Stop, in the name of all that's sane and insane (my mother's favorite phrase) before you turn into that man on the bus who does nothing but ride it all day and night, shitting in his pants and talking to himself. Before you turn into your idiotic Uncle Steve who doesn't even have a shirtsleeve to wipe his tears away. I look up at the painting of my childhood house that hangs above my bed.

I want to go back to that house and haunt it.

I call up my brother, who's dead. He was decapitated in a drunk driving accident when I was nine. Benson, I say. I'm sad and bored. Let's haunt the old house. *But you're alive,* he says. *How can you haunt a place when you're alive?* Don't be a retard, I say.

I meet my brother in the front yard of the old house. He is seventeen years old and has no head. You're looking pretty good, I say. I mean, considering. My big brother's ten years younger than me. He's still wearing the Violent Femmes T-shirt he wore the night of the crash. And he's got on blue Pro-Keds. The kind of sneakers Joanne Jett wore, as he always loved to proclaim. He's a handsome ghost, even without his head.

You look pretty good too, he says. *I see you've lost that weight.* It's true, I say, sort of proud. *How did you do it?* He asks. Oh, you know. I lost it a while ago. Mostly in college. Puking instead of eating. Drugs instead of puking. Drinking instead of drugs. Coffee instead of drinking. And now just a lot of coffee and swimming.

And I wonder how he really sees anything, since he has no eyes, and how he talks since he has no mouth, but I figure there are things about the afterlife I was never meant to understand.

The house looks like it did when we were kids. Except there are no skateboards, footballs, basketballs, horns, lunchboxes, bikes, Leggos, baseball gloves, sneakers or GI JOEs strewn about the lawn. The people who live here now are clearly better at living than we ever were. The bushes are all trimmed, the impatiens are in bloom, the driveway lights are working. We go into the house and all the way up to the third floor. My brother's lucky because he's dead. He floats and glows. I have to skip the fifth step because it creaks. Everyone in the house is sleeping and we don't want to wake them up.

This house gives me the creeps, Benson says. *Who would ever want to live here?*

The boy's room is dark, but we go inside anyway. I have to hide in the closet. *What's wrong with these kids,* he asks. *All they do is sleep.* It's nighttime, I say. *What's this kid's name?* The name Longstreet is sewn on to his sweaters. *That's a rough name,* he says.

So is Benson, I tell him. *And look what happened to me.*

The kid kicks a little in his sleep. He's sweating and moaning, just a little faintly in his dreams. I think you're giving him nightmares, I say to my brother. *But I'm not even saying anything. He doesn't even see me.* Maybe that's not how it works. We go around the house after that, not finding anything, not that I know what to look for. There are a few new lamps. The kitchen's yellow now. Lots of plants hanging from the ceiling. New paintings in the den. They've got a sheepdog that doesn't make a sound. We go from room to room, sort of quiet, making mental notes until we arrive at the front door again.

Well, this was the most boring thing I've ever done in my death, Benson says. *No offense. I'd better get going. It was good to see you, Sis. Although. I think you should decide in the morning whether you should get up or stay asleep. One or the other. The in-between life is beat.*

Sometimes I'd rather stay in my dreams, I tell him. *I know,* he says. *You don't have to tell me. I know,* and disappears without his head down the driveway, into the quiet street.

Music for the Still of the Night

This used to be my bedroom, but now it's the guest room, and my parents have taken away the glow-in-the-dark stars. It's the middle of the night, and I am back home, and I can't sleep because I can hear them in the next room. Tonight I realize my parents don't make love anymore. I can hear them actively *not* make love, lying awake next to each other under sheets, silent, my grey parents, stiff, and lumpy and alone.

Growing up, I heard them make love restlessly almost every night. Even during hard times in their marriage, even when my father threw a plant at my mother's head, even when my mother pulled a kitchen scissor on him, even when they called each other motherfucker and whore and bitch and bastard and jackass and cunt and fool, even when my mother screamed after him out the window in front of all of 7th Avenue, *go fuck yourself, egoist,* even when my father got down on his knees on the bathroom floor and cried, always at night they came together in bed, and made love like honeymooners, with tenderness, and ferocity, and abandon. I could hear it all. The grunts and the heaves and the moans and the sheets and the light laughter and the post-coital sighs.

When they weren't fighting, my parents were *that* couple: one hot afternoon unapologetically intertwined on the rocks in Central Park, necking, provoking glares from all the ladies with their tiny dogs and sighs from the barefoot teenage girls or *go for it, dude* from boys on skateboards in torn up pants. My father unbuttoned the top of her shirt, my mother bit his nose and I hid in the slide tower and hoped that they would stop.

But now in the middle of the night I hear them lying there without touching. Taking up space, breathing heavily but without a trace of passion. I am thirty years old, and I live at home and my parents have grown enormous. I do not understand how two such large people share the same bed. I'm amazed they are able to accomplish what humans accomplish. For instance, my mother plays the piano. My mother plays the piano every night before bed. She plays one piece, Beethoven's Pathetique, and it is exactly that, it is wrenching and sad, the piece itself, but also the way she has to hold herself up to play it, her largeness balancing on that tiny stool, and the way she plays it, so slowly, as though she has just learned it even though she has been playing it for years, she plucks the sadness right out of the piano, and it's impossible to listen to it and not go mad or not go straight to the liquor cabinet which I always do when I hear her play. I sit on the ottoman drinking Scotch and I listen and when she's through, she rises slowly, and I clap for her, and she says *oh really Donald stop* even though if she had her choice she would play for me all night because my father is so cruel, he doesn't have the patience to sit and listen and retreats to the bedroom when she plays. She could have been a musician, if only she'd learned more than one piece.

And right now, I can't get the piece out of my head and it is pulsing through my still drunk mind in time with my parents' non-lovemaking and the stale room is no help at all. I used to lie in this bed and gaze up at the stars. Now I'm gazing at paisley wallpaper the color of vomit. Now I'm inhaling the fumes of potpourri my father insists on stashing in the dresser drawers because he thinks it impresses people. Even though the jackass is allergic to it, and coughs and sneezes incessantly.

I haven't always lived here. I used to have a very exciting life of my own in Tenafly, New Jersey. I used to have high prospects, a paramour, a house with a gazebo. My wife and I would sit under the gazebo and talk for hours about absolutely nothing, and then we'd fuck, and talk and fuck and talk, one night until the sun rose and she looked at me, my love, bathed in light, she repeated these phrases that hypnotized me *where did you come from, I mean, where, where, where and god, I can't believe how time flies and you're so edible and how quiet the world is under a little round white roof with a bench, I absolutely adore you.*

They're awake, I know it. They're awake and waiting for morning. The feeling is awful and they've stopped fighting it. They don't stir or smoke. They just lie there not touching. In the morning, they'll forget about tonight's sleeplessness. They'll just move throughout the day, doing whatever it is two enormous old people do. Have their tea. Read the paper. Take their baths. They'll do everything in slow-motion, as though underwater. The underwater dance, I call it. The sleepwalk. The glazy eyed waltz. We are a family of insomniacs. Of drunks and coughers. Of before bed musicians. Of home-comers taking the train rides of shame to starless old bedrooms alone.

The cries come at dawn. When the room just begins to fill with light and I have just started to nod off. I don't get up when I hear them. Of course not, why would I, is it my business to run in and congratulate them, Mom and Dad, thank God you still have it in you, just when I thought romance had been sapped from the world. Instead I let them go on, I let them play a part in my dream. Because dreams are rare. I try not to think too much about the images the cries evoke. I never did. Even during puberty, I didn't actually imagine them in the act. But this morning, something about the physics of it, the purple elephants in the room, of course I have to imagine it, and really, what surprises me is that it doesn't disgust me, it really doesn't, but instead, I feel an intense happiness, and I curl up in my pillow and giggle into it in my half asleep state like a little boy. For once in my life, I feel safe again, and I have an enormous morning erection.

But they don't subside. And although at first I think it's because it's been so long, they are so hungry for each other, I realize soon that there is only one cry, and it isn't a cry, it is deeper than that. More intense, more guttural, more from the stomach. It is one wail, and one weeping. One is my father, and the other is my mother and it's the weeping that does it. The weeping wakes me up, shakes me from the fantasy, but I do not move. She does not call my name, and when they ask me why I didn't come, I'll just say you never called my name, you old fools, you old fat fools, you driveling lonely fuckheads, you didn't call my name, how was I supposed to know, what was I supposed to think, you have your own lives, for years I've lived away from you, what am I always supposed to look after you, is that my job as your son, am I supposed to come running at the mere sound of cries and weeps, am I supposed to interrupt my sleep to check on some morning crying, how am I supposed to know you aren't just fucking, BESIDES YOU NEVER CALLED MY NAME! I hide under the pillow to block out the sounds. I taste the pillow. I bite into the down. But they don't subside, they don't weaken or fade, they get stronger, they get stronger and I stand up and my erection has subsided but the cries haven't and I go. I am drunk still. I am drunk, the cries. My mother, the weeps. The floor, the potpourri. Beethoven. Beethoven. Where are my stars? The doorknob. Do I knock? Mom. He has fallen off the bed, the slippery old whale. It's his back. It's his back. Mom, Mom.

My mother on her hands and knees, my father on his back next to her wailing, his face dry, but the sound escaping, only once before I saw him cry, no a thousand times I saw him cry and each time was like the first. You are too old for crying, mister. *Donald, the phone,* my mother says. Where have they put it? By the dresser. Oh god I stumble over slippers and a pile of books. The radio alarm goes off, the phone I forget how to use it, the buttons light, I touch the numbers and how to speak we need an ambulance right now please my voice calm have I grown old my father's pleading he moves his mouth is he asking a question, what does he need. Spit escapes. I stand over them. My mother holds a tissue from her eyes to his lips. Together we do not touch him.

Send

Dear Janine:

You think I don't listen, but it's not true. I listen. Tonight I listened. I went to the bathroom and sat on the toilet. I put my ear to the wall. He felt me listening. I listened to him feel me listening. In his room, lying on his bed. He didn't shout at me or hit the wall with his fist. He didn't ignore me and try to fall asleep. He sighed loudly. If I stayed out there all night he'd sigh like that every ten minutes until the sun came up and what do you think that would do? I listened to the sound of his feet pacing his room, to his body flopping back onto the mattress. To his restlessness, his heaviness. I listened to him breathing and reading. I held my breath so he wouldn't hear me listening. But he hears everything. The kid's like me, he never sleeps. All he does is read.

Dear Paul:

If you have something to say to me, why don't you say it to my face? I've had enough of this absolutely ludicrous behavior. I am so sick of you moping around this house like some sort of anguished wounded elephant. You treat this house like it's a hotel. How do you think your mother feels, watching you act this way? She's at a total loss. Her sadness is unbearable and I have to sleep next to it every night. I can feel you seething every time we cross paths. What is wrong with you? Why don't you get a summer job? It's the middle of July already. Anything, anything will do. Sling coffee, sell shoes, mow a goddamn lawn. You're eighteen and that's too old for this goofing around. Is it you can't handle the world? It's too big and makes you sad. It makes me sad too. It's a big sad world and we live in it. We eat dinner watching. But for now let's not dwell on unpleasant things. Let's not act like complete morons. Let's talk for once in our lives.

How many times have I told you to call your uncle to see if he will hire you for the summer? It doesn't have to be for the rest of your life. Tell me how many times I've asked you. I think it's time you shape up your act or found your own place. Why don't you talk to your sister when she comes home, if she ever comes home? She seems to know what she's doing. Also, there is a reason God invented doorknobs.

Dear Ruth:

Why don't you give us a call? It's terrible that you never call home. How do we know you haven't been abducted? I understand your pathological desire to live in the eye of the storm, but I'll tell you what's been happening at home since you've been in Iraq, Iran, Swaziland, Afghanistan, the Sudan, and Haiti. Your brother has grown into an elephant. I don't mean he's become fat, although he has—he has grown fat with sadness. He's driving us all completely out of our minds. He is reading Les Chants de Maldoror, the homicidal flying beast. The thirsty demon who carries hearts in his mouth while sobbing his sorrowful dirge. Tonight I stole the book from him and I've been trying to read it myself. This creature carries brains around on his beard and rapes children and spouts out ideas about the universe. And all of that is not supposed to make him weird? I don't mind the moping. I mind the secret boiling behind his forehead. He read at the dinner table tonight, chewing his meatballs in small mouthfuls, not once looking up from the pages. I watched the trouble in his eyes for almost an hour. Your mother watched me watch him.

He also has a habit of smoking on the roof and throwing the cigarette butts onto the lawn. Your mother and I have raised a pig. A pig who smokes.

Dear Janine:

I'm tired of hearing about your illnesses. Nobody is healthier than you. Real people are suffering, real pain exists. Don't you read the paper or care about anybody but yourself? What about our daughter who is living in the middle of it, surrounded by detonating corpses this week, beheadings that week, and entire villages of parentless children next week? And I have to hear about your anxious paranoid hallucinations of sickness. And the way you talk to me, it's as though I'm not really here. It's as though I've died and you are walking around like some insane widow, talking to my ghost.

Dear Paul:

What do I find every morning before work? Cigarette butts, ashes on my lawn. Thrown off the roof by whom? This is the thanks I get for allowing you to eat my food and pace my hallways. A boy of your girth shouldn't be smoking. A smoker shouldn't be so fat. If you're so interested in morbidity, you should know what is bad for your health.

Dear Ruth:

Your mother may have a serious illness. I think it's just migraines, but who knows? How would you feel if a scan came back and a giant tumor was growing in her brain? What would you do then? Would you lecture us on the wrongness of war? Would you send us another joke about the president? What kind of daughter lets her parents and her little brother die? You think you're brilliant and some sort of ethical genius, but you've never learned any responsibility. And stop sending us those horrific photographs. We've stopped reading the paper for a reason. We're through with politics. We hate the world. We've had enough of it. Here is a fact: you hate the president more than you love us. That's the only thing in the world that's certain. I don't want to hear about the people you've met. You might as well have murdered us, the way you pretend we don't exist. I'm ashamed of you. I hope you never come home. Call us immediately or we'll call the embassy.

Dear Janine:

I don't want to hear your voice. We have a serious issue on our hands. The issue is our son. What about all those shootings they keep talking about on the radio? Have you been into his room? Have you ever wondered what you'd do if you found something under his bed? A gun or something worse? Don't you know he may be dying in that little room of his? Don't you think maybe his sadness isn't all that normal? I wonder if tonight will be the night I find him in a bath full of blood, his brains all over the side of the tub. Or if he will jump off the roof. Or if he will take pills that make his heart stop. In the morning, I will read the note he will have left. I will look at it and not be able to read. I will never read anything ever

*again. Not the paper, not street signs. I honestly don't
know what you've been up to for the past fifteen years.
Sleeping, probably.*

Dear Paul:

*It's not that we don't love Ruth, it's just that I
don't understand why she feels the need to go to these
places, like she's an action hero. And why does she fall in
love with crazy people like that? I have no problem with
the fact that she loves women. I have a problem with the
nasty people she chooses as her partners. A drunk, a thief,
a lying sociopath? If I had lovers like that, I'd run to the
other side of the planet myself. Why does she love them?*

Dear Janine:

*If only our lives were like the movies. After he'd
had enough of hearing me spy on him, he would open
the door slowly. He would look at me, and I would look
at him, and after a pause he would offer me a cigarette,
and we would go up the hallway ladder to the roof to
smoke. We'd smoke up there, watching the green line of
sunrise. After crying over the planet, he'd tell me about
his real problems: a girl he loves, some gangly thing that
is crushing his heart, that's chewing him up into pulpy
bits and spitting him out through her teeth, and I would
offer him my sleeve for his tears. I'd say, there's only one
thing you need to know about girls…and I would know
the secret and I would whisper it and he would look at
me, changed.*

Or maybe we would fight like men. I'd kick down that door and bust into the room I haven't entered in years. I'd throw a few punches at the memory of acne on that face. He'd kick my stomach. I'd wrestle him to the floor. He'd spit. I'd beat his forehead. This is my hand. This is life. It stinks like blood and burning hearts. It doesn't care if you're sad. Live, die, and it's still there. Get used to it. Nothing changes for a thousand years.

Dear Ruth:

I can't sleep. I toss in my sheets for hours, staring at the molding on the ceiling. There is a pale giant moon outside our window and it floods the room with too much light. The night crickets are slowly driving me nuts. Your mother is asleep and I don't want to wake her. Why is it none of this crosses my mind during the day? I go to work, sit in the park with my coffee at lunch, I eat dinner without thinking, and then when it's time to turn in, all this stupidity rushes in. It is so hot this summer. Dogs are dehydrating in Harlem apartments. A whole family in Staten Island woke up dead. The air conditioner is broken.

Dear Night:

Stop worrying, crazy. Stop thinking about what isn't. He is who he is. He feels what he feels. Let him feel it himself. If he wants to tell you, he'll tell you. When he's ready, he'll tell you. Tell me what? His heart's broken. The air conditioner's broken. The whole world is broken.

He doesn't know what he wants. What do you want? I wish I could hit you, hold your head to the toilet. I wish I could hang you upside down from the roof and shake some life into you. There was a time when I held him back with my hands. Look, I said. Look at the glass you broke. Look at the boy you hurt. Look at the dumbness in this math homework. Does that look like a seven to you? Open your eyes. Does that look like two thirds? Look at your knees, for Christ's sake. Look at your cage of a room. You live in this slop? A gorilla couldn't live here.

Dear Paul:

I have nothing new to say to you. But there are so many things that have been said that need to be said over and over again. Don't think I don't know how maddening the world is. I think about it every night before I go to bed. If you think I haven't thought about checking out a little early myself, you're absolutely wrong. I once had the urge to jump off the Verrazano Narrows Bridge. I slowed down traffic, I looked down at the boats from the window, but I didn't have the guts to get out of the car.

Your sister has guts but she cannot stay in one place. I wonder sometimes if she stayed what she would feel. If she sat and watched instead of sending those photos out into the night. If she looked at them and saw them.

Dear Janine:

Not just night. During the day sometimes. Not his voice, but the sound of him.

Dear Paul:

It's because we were too hard on you when you were young and too easy on you later. My father was the same way with me. If you have a son, you'll be the same way with him.

Dear Night:

And what am I supposed to make of the monster in this book? Sometimes I feel like he is watching me read his words. He is outside the window, peering into the bedroom. He hangs from the roof by his feet. He tries to be quiet, but how can something that enormous be quiet? What does he think of me and why does he care? And am I supposed to feel sorry for him for committing those massacres?

Dear Janine:

My concern is that I've somehow lost track, that at a certain point I stopped knowing her. And that now she is on the global search for hell. Undoubtedly she's found it everywhere she's gone. But it isn't enough to find it. She must live there, in the center of it, until she is part of the flames.

Dear Ruth:

Talk to your little brother when you come home. Tell him something. Talk to him about what you do. That eventually you did something and that now you are fine, or at least that you are looking for something. Make him understand life doesn't just happen, that it doesn't just descend upon you that you have to stand up at some point, stand up and do something. You don't understand how serious it is. He's reading Maldoror, and you know you have your mother to blame for that. He's spending ridiculous amounts of time in his room. It isn't just one thing, it's a thousand things. It's a universe of things. Whatever it is, I don't know what it is, it doesn't have a name. Whatever it is, it's terrible and he won't talk to me. He won't talk to your mother. He should be out getting laid, or at least talking to people. I don't even know what to say to him. It's terrible to worry like this. It's not good for my heart. I'm not young anymore. You'll have to face that soon. The fact that I'm not young anymore is one of life's horrible realities.

When you get home, teach your little brother to turn the doorknob when he closes the door.

Dear Janine:

I would write him a letter, but what would I say in the letter? I want to tell him a secret, ask him a question, give him some good advice. I want to write the letter on thick paper and I want to fold it carefully and put it in an envelope and I want to lick that envelope and slip it under the door so that later he will sit in a quiet place and hold the words in his hands and speak them as he reads them. And when he is done reading the letter, he will fold it into a tiny square and put it in his pocket with his keys, his knives, his Chapstick, whatever he keeps in his pocket.

Before he falls asleep, he will read my words again in bed, and again in the morning with his coffee. This will be a beautiful letter. I'll write it with a fountain pen.

Dear Ruth:

We don't have any fountain pens in this house. Only blue ballpoint pens chewed on the ends, stuffed in the Mike's Pipe Yard mug that's been sitting on that desk since the beginning of time. None of those pens even write anymore, but your mother keeps them around to hold us under the illusion that there are pens in this house that work.

Dear Mug:

You, and everything I'd love to throw out this window. If only my hands were big enough to hold all the things I'd love to hurl off the rooftop, into the night. Our coat racks, our lampshades, our toothbrushes, the iron, the candles, the spoons, the jar of cashews, the milk, the violin, the television, the boots, the air conditioner, the figurines above the fireplace, the maps, the board games, the humidifier, the books, the plastic folding chairs, the breakfast table, the roller skates, the glue gun, the juggling balls, the rabbit cages, the sock drawers, the maple syrup, the ashtrays, the photo frames, the sheet music, the dog dishes, the erasers, the sponges, the potted midnight fichus, the refrigerator magnets, the tuxedo, the striped apron, the wolf mask, the Q-tips, the hammer, the dental floss, her yellow evening dress, the bracelets, the swimming goggles, the paperclips, the sea monkeys, the stockings, the clocks, the bean bags, the frozen meat, the cotton, the newspaper, our bathrobes, the pennies, the aspirin, the dishrags, the cans of tomato juice, the old rug in the hallway, the cords, the shoelaces, the guitar strings, the doorknobs, the eggs, the cigarettes, the hair bands, the records, the soaps, the cutting board, the bags of salt in the basement, the champagne corks, and all the broken useless pens sticking up inside of you.

Dear Paul:

Your mother is naked right now. She never slept naked when she was beautiful. When she was beautiful she hid herself in saggy pajamas with horrible things like penguins on them. Now one giant alabaster leg crosses over the other, so pale it's almost blue. A fly rests on her forehead, but she doesn't lift a finger to scratch it. I listen to her sleep and dream. Listen to her breathe. Our bodies are close, but we do not touch with the heat. I'm jealous of sleep like that. Her head hits the pillow and she's gone. When she wakes up in the morning, she wants to talk to me about nonsense. How she hurts, but there is nothing hurting her. A spot on her hand makes her head spin. She is getting old, that's true, but it's oldness of the mind. I remember when she loved the world. She doesn't read the paper anymore. She says she can't read it. She only reads novels and talks to me about her dreams. She doesn't want to talk about anything important. She leaves the teakettle on, leaves her keys at work every other day, leaves the bathroom a mess with her hairs.

Dear Ruth:

Yesterday she said I was the one who's lost my mind, the one who doesn't want to look at anything. She speaks to me sometimes like she is seven years old, doing the dishes barefoot, watering the driveway flowers. I answer her like an adult. Do not talk to me about all of that, I tell her. The past may as well be a dream. But she goes on about it. She asks me to remember. She isn't a parent. She lets him get away with murder. Lets him read at the dinner table and stay out at all hours. What does he do out there? He doesn't have any friends.

Dear Paul:

Is it the world you are afraid of? Why do you spend so many nights awake? Why can't you close your eyes and dream? Don't you think it would be nice to not carry the world around, to just go away into yourself?

Dear Night:

It begins in the bedroom. Janine and I are talking, we are getting ready for bed. It feels strangely undreamlike, except there is an odd breeze. Her hair blows. There is a little rattling on the windows. We fight over who will go downstairs and get glasses of water. It is a pleasant fight. She throws a pillow at me and we laugh.

Dear Paul:

It's one thing to worry about your self. But what about when it's someone else's worry that drags your feet and goes into your head and keeps you up at night? I'll get over my own worries, like the fact that in thirty years, I'll probably be dead. Can you imagine what it would be like to watch all your friends die? But this kind of worry isn't good for my health. There is nothing I can do. I have to teach you the worst lesson, but I don't even know how to teach it to you, or what it is. I don't understand what the lesson is. How do I tell you anything?

Dear Night:

We hear him in the hallway. His door closes. We don't understand what he's doing there, just standing outside our door. We look at each other as we hear him run down the stairs. My wife says to me: Go now.

Dear Ruth:

I don't have to tell him. His gut already knows. You must come home. But when you come home, you must stop falling in love with these maniacs.

Dear Night:

I pause for a moment at the door. My back hurts, a shooting pain from my ankles to the tip of my spine. And I have a thought: I shouldn't be doing this. But I go on, through the door. I follow him down the quiet street, but I do not want to catch up with him. I do not know what to say to him. I've never known. There are no cars. The lights are off in all the houses. It's as though everybody left this town years ago. Left their houses and their gates swinging open. The crickets are deafening. He has headphones on, so he doesn't hear me follow him. He is enormous, five times the size he really is. The streetlights make his shadow longer. A bag is slung across his shoulder and it flaps at his hip. He picks up his gait to a slow jog. We go down the street into the night. He stops for a moment at the hill and looks up, the silhouette of him at the edge of the street. He goes on. He runs faster. I try and catch up, but I don't want to catch up. I want him to see me and I do not want him to see me. Even in my dream I have nothing to say to him. I never did.

I left the house with no shoes, but now I'm wearing sneakers. They take the weight off my feet, make me float on the pavement. The giant moon still glows, but I can feel the morning. And it's very awful. It's a cold morning and it's coming. The thought of the day makes me sick. I feel sick to my stomach and I start to lose my footing. I feel something move in my gut, like my stomach is eating itself. I put my hand under my shirt to stop it, but my hand goes away. It is there but made of nothing. I'm not in shape for running. I vomit air all over the sidewalk, but I don't even stop, I go on. Terrible things rush through my head. What he could do out here in this quiet. Maybe something is in the bag. Drugs or razor blades or something worse. He will blow something up. Set everything on fire. But I know it's worse than that. Pieces of himself. His flesh cut up into squares. How will I put them together? He is running away. He will get on a bus, go to the city, live on the streets, eat out of trashcans, but it is worse than that, he will slowly disappear.

My teeth swell. My cheeks are full of sand. We come to the woods, three miles from our house.

Dear Janine:

It's time to talk now. It's time to say, tell me what's new. Or what the hell's wrong with us, why aren't we sleeping? Who came in here at night and stole our sleep? But it's quiet and almost morning. Another scorcher. This is the summer that never ends. I'd give anything to have night again. To have the whole night to sleep.

Dear Night:

The trees are covered with mosquitoes. Gnats swarm above the black pond. But it is only a pond. The water doesn't move. He stands on the rock that juts out into the pond. I stand behind a tree, watching my son on the rock. He slips out of his sandals. He takes off his shirt. He closes his eyes. He takes an audible breath. The sky lights up: pink and green smoke. I open my mouth. He opens his wings and flies.

Dear Beast:

Look what you've done. If you think I'll ever forgive you, you're wrong. I hate all your stories and all your songs. Your wings are so broken, they don't even cast a shadow on my rooftop. Your explanations and philosophies and theoretical ramblings are a waste of my time. You think you're some sort of artist? Not one soul is moved by any of your work. I hate what you do every night of your life. You have the right to feel lonely. Not one person empathizes. There is not a single tear shed in your direction. The night hates you, my family hates you, the moon hates you, the ink of this pen hates you, the streets and the houses and all the crickets hate you. All the sleepless dead in all of history are standing in their bedrooms, singing. They all wish you would choke on your own prey, on your own snot and saltwater and hideous laughter. You're a complete embarrassment, a complete and total failure. You are not even worth the paper this tiny letter is written on. And who writes letters with pens and paper anymore? Who sits and reads shaky handwriting?

What have I lost? Tell me. An entire night of my life, every single person I have ever or will ever love, millions of words, a billion breaths, countless indelible moments, every one of my hairs, and who knows how many dreams. The person who's reading this is probably already dead or else salvaging paper from the recycling bin at the edge of the driveway. Murder is one thing, but look what you've done to my lawn. How can I look out my window? Paper all over. Scraps and leftovers. Not even the birds will eat them. Nobody will send these idiotic letters. Nobody will read them. And who will have to clean up that mess in the morning? I will, you

son of a bitch—the paper, the ashes, the pens, the brains,
the hearts, all by myself before work, the whole fucking
mess.

Electra

Let's just say she couldn't stop dreaming of her father and brother. The guts of those dreams, how often they occurred, how her body thrashed or stayed so still it scared the mice…or how those dreams began and ended, the hands and mouths and lips and stomachs, the friction versus flow, which came first the wetness or the rage, we'll let stay in the shadows. And when the thought of plunging the sword into her mother's chest crept in, the spigot of life from her step Dad's neck, every other stop on the subway, deep in the night when sleep wouldn't come, her heart got stuck. No love could shift it.

The Gods knew there was no justice in that world, only bad haircuts and dreams of boats and blood. So when she walked to the top of the mountain and knelt to them, when she hit the stick on the sacred ground and sang to them, when she spilled her jug of sorrows, *I'm on my knees, Apollo, my mother put me on this earth to die, she opened her legs to death, Thy will be done, Oh Gods*, drunk on it, bursting, the gleaming shift in her eyes, the lilt of that prayer, nothing came back: only carrion birds, the empty chatter of friends, those faithful slaves, the clouds.

Still, she wanted.

Her brother's hopes were quieter—an image here, a breath there, a guilty dream tucked into sleep. Mostly he still loved Helen, born from an egg, the whore who sparked it all. Such are the lives of the dumb and vanquished. Or of the young.

Should we go with them into the hut? Hear the break of her mother's ribcage and the screams that followed? Dare we cut to the scene of that crime? Or shall we send the messenger? He was always a good one for speeches, ugly as he was. A good one for holding intestines in his hands. He knew what to tell and what to hide away, which details were worth repeating. For instance, was it clear they had fucked that night? Did her mother sleep on his aging chest? Was there one pillow or two? Could the affair have been its own chaotic mess, one drawn out punishment, full of nasty fights, defenestrated possessions, alarm clocks, photo frames, wine glasses, all broken on the street, or worse, silent, the minutes and the hours and the years? Had the night of their murders been the first night of love's trembling doubt, in which she asked herself for the first time at dinner, worrying the tablecloth, over meatloaf and peas, *for this, for this, my life for this?*

The teenagers' red stained shirts as they exited the hut. Quiet on the set. The oracles arrived on chariots, blinding the chorus and the players, and the audience. Better never than late. Still more speeches.

Must we listen? Must we suffer through the slow sonata of the verdict? Will we sit and listen to those tired lists? Who will protest? Who will leave the theater? Who will spit at all those cynical crooks, the all-knowing knuckleheads playing chess, feigning rage and disappointment while laughing, breathlessly laughing?

All this, as you know, has already been written: the need, the blood, the banishment. So out they went, the murderers, as ordered, side by side, too old to forget, too young to wander the wine dark sea.

If You Want to be Happy
for the Rest of Your Life

Now that my wife walked out, now that my brother is dead and there is nobody left to think I'm ridiculous, I think I will marry Alice. From where I stand tonight under the street lamp, in the quietest part of this sleepless city, I can tell we would make the perfect match. She is enormous, and she is made of stone and she faces the sailboat pond and she holds a book on her lap and for the rest of eternity, when all of us are covered in worms, when this fascinating historical moment has come to a gradual *ritardando,* when we've all been assassinated, when the levies break, and the buildings collapse, and when there is nothing left of our astonishing stories but falling paper, she will, under rubble, under water, under rotting corpses, under the starless sky and the rustling leaves, and the silence that follows gunshots and finales, persist to read this book.

Exeunt

Your oldest will fall down the front door steps one icy night. He'll hit his head on the steel banister. His wife will find him in the morning, his front teeth on the first step, blood against snow, his body large in pajamas. She'll be holding her coffee, nursing a hangover from the night before, when she was too gone to notice he had not been there in bed next to her. She'll stumble outside, hoping to find him shoveling the walkway. There he'll lie: his head turned to the side the way you remember him as an infant in his crib.

Your youngest son, he'll not know when to stop. He'll be thirty years old, that athletic body you remember, you stared at, you wanted all for yourself. The shoulders of a soldier. He'll dance himself to death the way they did in the old days, the old myths, the women who danced to their deaths, he will collapse like them, your youngest, a slave to the beat. Four o'clock in the morning at a warehouse club, his heart will stop in the thick of sweat, between two bodies grinding.

A tumor will develop behind your daughter's left earlobe. She will lose her hearing, her sight, her sense of smell. Dysphasia. And this will kill her husband. The ends of sentences and the meanings of words. At ninety-three, she will totter to the sink. She will stumble over to the bed some night remembering mumbling riddles and her husband will also want to go there, *go there, take me with you, into the you part, the darkened secrets wasn't there a summertime camp song the wet leaves of almost morning and can I hold your hand and we have lived hard on this beach of rock and bird bone, and will you kiss it and will you place it on my knee and sing.*

Acknowledgments

Very special thanks to Michelle Carter, Peter Orner, Toni Mirosovich, Micheline Aharonian Marcom, and Rick Moody for so much generous support, inspiration, and encouragement; the Creative Writing department at San Francisco State University; competition judge Mikhail Iossel; Maria Suarez and the Fourteen Hills staff; the Wood family; and to LP for coming to my birthday party and putting up with the mess.

About the Author

Anne-E. Wood has an MFA in Fiction from San Francisco State University. Her work has appeared in *Beloit Fiction Journal, the Licking River Review, Other Voices, The Cream City Review, Fiction Attic,* and *Fourteen Hills.* She is the Associate Artistic Director of Performing Arts Workshop in San Francisco, where she teaches Creative Writing and Theater in public schools and at juvenile hall.